DRAGONPETS

The Sacrifice

R.L.S. HOFF

The Pencil Princess Workshop

For Katie, with love

Map of Heshal & Arkon

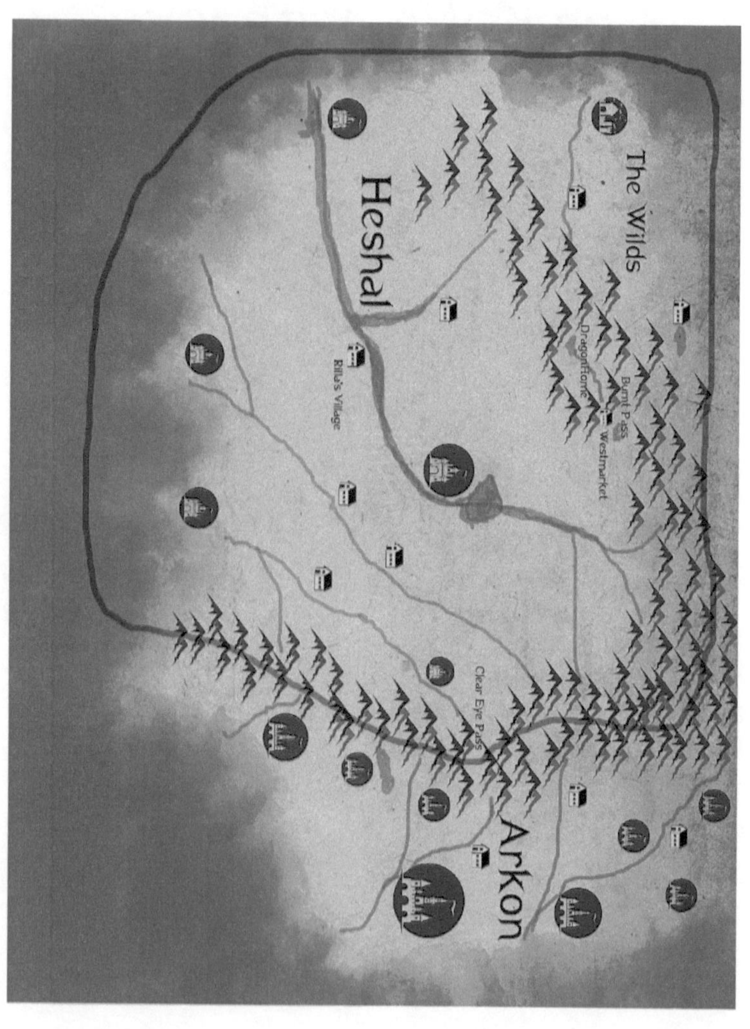

CHAPTER ONE

Missing Memories

I should have been worried about the dragon.

A cold gust of wind snatched my breath away. The chains that shackled me to the iron loop in the rock ledge above my head rattled at my futile effort to free myself. The clanging echoed, but brought only noise, not freedom. My mind felt muddled, thick with a weary haze that wouldn't clear.

I couldn't find the will to try any harder. I wondered at my lethargy. It wasn't like me, and neither was the flimsy finery I'd let the giggling palace girls talk me into wearing. Why had I agreed to don this ridiculous ball gown, again? My thoughts felt sluggish, and my memory seemed foggy. Was it the drink they'd given me before I dressed? Or could Sir Drake have pressed some mind magic on me to make me docile?

I shuddered.

Even if I'd been drugged and magically quieted, why hadn't I insisted on my own clothes? I'd known they were readying me for this, to be sacrificed, left in the mountains for the dragon. Surely, I wasn't fool enough to imagine the bright silk and intricate lace would provide protection against the whistling wind and high altitude.

The magician's soldiers had only been gone minutes before I longed for my comfortable woolen dress and thick homespun shawl.

Now, I couldn't even remember what had happened to them, and the more I thought about it, the more the memories slipped from my grasp, like an unruly piglet beneath my fingers.

Not knowing where my clothes had gone didn't bother me so much, but some of the other holes in my memory disturbed me. I remembered my home, the farm on the side of the hill, with the squat thatch-roofed buildings and smell of manure. I also remembered the airy palace of cool pink marble, but try as I might, I couldn't recall how I'd gone from the one to the other. That bit of memory was gone, and I couldn't help poking at it the way my little brothers always poked with their tongues at the holes left after teeth came out.

Two threads of steam slipped from the cave in front of me, thickened, merged, and filled the whole mountain dell.

Relief sagged through me, though part of me realized that smoke meant the dragon was getting closer.

Steam curled around me, and I couldn't help appreciating the warmth. My fingers and toes screamed as sensation returned to them, but I'd felt worse after Twelfth-month mornings milking the cows, and I knew I'd retain the use of them all.

Well, I would if I lived long enough, which didn't seem likely. What did it matter if a sacrifice could feel her fingers? She'd hardly need them tomorrow. I laughed, and the sound echoed, growing raucous and insane as it bounced across the valley and back. Why had I agreed to this again? There was a reason, I knew, but like my memory of going to the palace, it eluded me.

It seemed unnatural, the way my mind skimmed over these things, as if it had been altered, though I couldn't imagine why anyone would have bothered to tinker with my memories. Why Sir Drake would have bothered. After all, he was the only magician powerful enough to tinker with my memories so. But why would he want to spend his precious magical energy altering the mind of a country girl destined to be set out like a cow for a dragon?

Yet, something blocked me from my own mind. It was a puzzle so engrossing that I didn't see the long black snout poking out of the cave until it jerked in my direction, and the dragon captured me with its emerald gaze.

Such beautiful eyes for such a horrible beast. I knew I should look away. Everyone always said it was death to get trapped in a dragon's mesmerizing stare, but it was too late now, and besides, what difference would it make? I was already on the menu.

The dragon chuckled. Then it flashed forward so quickly that I saw nothing but a blur until its hot scales pressed against me. The creature coiled around me, squeezing between me and the rock wall at my back and then circling around to my front. I squeaked, sounding frightened even to my own ears as it looped about me twice more, enclosing me so that I could not move. I felt no pain, however, not even from the claw that rested on my right shoulder, nor from the one that lifted my chin so that I had no choice but to stare up the long black snout into the beast's eyes.

In my mind, a deep musical voice thrummed, *What are you doing here? Where's my cow?*

How could he talk to me in my head that way?

Fool! I'm a dragon. This is how we speak. Now where's my cow?

"Your cow? I'm the sacrifice this year. You'd rather have a cow?"

The dragon snorted, and steam billowed at me, hot, though no hotter than what came off a pot when I lifted the lid to see how the porridge was faring. This steam was thicker, though, and for a moment, I couldn't see the dragon's eyes. I glanced down. When the air cleared, I noticed a golden choker around the dragon's neck before the claw under my chin forced my gaze back to the dragon's eyes. They glittered, and the voice in my mind took on a commanding tone. *Tell the truth!*

My whole body stiffened at the command, but as I knew nothing more about cow sacrifices than I did before, all I could say was, "I don't know anything about a cow."

The green eyes above me seemed to grow larger until they were all I could see, my whole world. *You believe this to be true—but not all of you.*

"Excuse me?" I fought to keep my voice steady.

Part of you knows, but the knowledge has been hidden from your awareness. Do I have permission to enter fully into your mind and look for the answers I seek?

"You need my permission?"

The dragon snorted again. This time the fog that passed before my eyes was brief, and when it cleared away, the dragon's eyes had returned to their normal size. *I do not need your permission, but I want it. If I must force my way into your mind, the process will be much more painful for you, and I would not hurt you more than I must. But I will use force if I have to. I need to know what Sir Drake is plotting against me.*

"Sir Drake? I can't imagine that the king's magician would have confided in me."

Ah, but who else could have locked your own thoughts away from you?

I considered my slippery memory. Perhaps the dragon was right. "I agree," I whispered, closing my eyes. "Do what you need to do."

Look at me. The musical tones sounded almost sorry for me.

I opened my eyes and stared directly into his deep green ones. They expanded again until it seemed that I floated inside a sea of green. A soft touch, like a silken thread, wound sinuously through my head, and where it touched, memories flared—the smell of my mother's bread fresh from the oven, the fiery light of a new day, the touch of my baby brother's hand in mine, the feel of mud between my toes as I stood on the bank of the stream next to the

Upper Fields. Then there was a blankness, a lack where there ought to have been something.

"What is that?" I whispered.

This is going to hurt, I'm afraid.

"What? NO!"

A flash of white-hot pain ripped through my skull, and memories roared in, like water over a cliff. For a moment, I was back at the farm, standing in the woods with a basket of freshly picked mushrooms over one arm, when a great purple beast dove from the skies, burning all before it. The fields smoked. The house, stable, barns, and chicken coop roared with flame so fierce that my mother and youngest siblings had no chance to escape. Nor could the horses and pigs get out. I would hear the mingled screams of people and animals and smell the sick-sweet smell of burning flesh from now until the end of time. Or I would if no one locked the memories away from me again.

I'd run toward the house that day, knowing even as I ran that I would be too late, that no one could possibly get out, but something in me wouldn't let me give up hope.

Out of the corner of my eye, I saw something moving in the field. Before I could fully comprehend what I was seeing, the dragon plunged, faster than an arrow, and swallowed my eldest brother whole. There wasn't time for Khan to yell out in either anger or fear before he disappeared inside the dragon's maw.

My father screamed. Roaring like an enraged beast and waving a pitchfork, he hobbled toward the purple beast.

The dragon laughed with a deep, earth-shaking sound that froze me where I stood, but Papa kept moving. The dragon swiped a claw at him, knocking the pitchfork into the next field. Then Papa followed Khan into the beast's maw.

At that, Lark, my elder by less than a year, squealed like a stuck pig and ran for the forest. The dragon swallowed him before he even made it out of the fields. The screams from the house and barns stopped, and heat rose all around me.

I stood amongst the wreckage of my home and wondered why I was still alive.

The dragon turned toward me as if summoned by my thoughts. It leapt into the air, spread its wings, and alighted in front of me, fixing me with obsidian eyes.

"Never look a dragon in the eye," Papa had always said. "It will be the last thing you do."

In that moment, I hoped he was right.

The dragon laughed again. The ground trembled beneath me, and though I struggled to stay upright, I refused to bend before this monster.

Well, you're a feisty one, aren't you? Pretty, too. I believe I'll keep you.

"You'll do nothing of the sort," I said. The tremors in my voice sounded pathetic, but at least I was speaking.

Ah, little one, who will stop me?

The dragon breathed on me, my feet buckled beneath me, and I remembered no more until I woke wearing strange nightclothes in a fancy bed in the palace.

CHAPTER TWO

The Palace

At the palace, pretty girls in fancy dresses fussed over me, telling me how Sir Drake and his men had found me in the clutches of a dragon and rescued me, but the beast had escaped. Sir Drake had a plan, though.

When I first woke, I couldn't remember the slaughter at the farm, so I asked about my family, but the girls only looked away and changed the subject. Their reluctance to speak of the matter triggered my suspicions and brought the memory of the dragon attack back in full force. My family was gone—Mama, the girls, and the baby caught in the house, Khan, Lark and Papa eaten by the dragon.

"Sir Drake said she would not remember," the girl in pink whispered.

"Then Sir Drake was wrong," I said.

All three girls gasped as if I spoke some heresy.

I rolled my eyes. "When can I return to my farm?"

The girl in yellow patted my hand, and the one in white said, "poor thing."

"I'll be much better when I return," I said.

"You can't," Yellow Girl said.

"It's still smoking," White Girl added.

"And it's not your farm any longer, is it?" Pink Girl said. "Girls can't inherit. Unless one of your brothers survived?"

I sank into the cushions that had been piled behind me on the bed. "No. All my brothers died in the attack."

"Perhaps an uncle?" White Girl suggested.

I shook my head. "I have no uncles."

"Then the land goes to the crown," Pink Girl said.

How convenient for the crown. I knew emissaries from the king had often visited our village these past several months, looking to purchase land on the cheap for a new highway. They threw their weight around, but when Papa had reminded our neighbors that by law, no man could be forced to give up his holdings, and certainly not for a pittance, none had sold.

They'd probably all sold now—or even given their lands away. No one would want to stay in a dragon's hunting grounds. The king would get his highway, and for even less than the minuscule recompense originally offered. If it weren't patently ridiculous, I might believe the king was in league with the dragon.

No dragon would submit to a merely human king, though, and no king of any intelligence at all would trust a dragon.

"Are you all right?" Yellow Girl asked.

"I think I'd like to be alone if you don't mind," I said. It wouldn't do to have any of them guessing at my traitorous thoughts, though, honestly, what more could they do to me? My family was gone, and my farm stolen.

"Sir Drake said we mustn't," White Girl said. "He says we must take great care of the woman who is to be his bride."

"His what?" I shrieked.

"His bride," Pink Girl said, "though I don't know what he sees in you."

"Alvina!" Yellow Girl hissed and bustled Pink Girl from the room.

White Girl patted my hand. "You mustn't mind Alvina. She's a bit testy because, of course, she wanted Sir

Drake for herself, and, until you came along, she was the prettiest single lady here. She can't help but be jealous."

I tried to smile at the girl, but I'm not sure I succeeded. "Thank you, though I don't think I'm all that pretty, and I'm sure I don't want to marry anyone." Especially the king's magician. Every story I'd heard about Sir Drake suggested the man was powerful, but cruel.

"Oh, but you must! It's so romantic. He saved you from that awful beast."

"The dragon who killed my family?"

"Yes."

"I thought you said it escaped."

"It did, but Sir Drake is the one who chased it off."

"It'll be back," I said. "It told me it meant to keep me." Everybody knew that the only way to permanently separate a dragon from treasure it had claimed was by killing the dragon.

White Girl's eyes widened, and she yelped. "That's terrible! We must tell Sir Drake!" She grabbed me by the hand and dragged me from the bed, out of the room, down a long pink marble hall, up three broad steps and down a twisty white marble corridor. She halted before a broad double door and pounded on the intricately carved oak. "Sir Drake! Sir Drake! Oh, you must see us. The dragon is coming here!"

~ 10 ~

CHAPTER THREE

Sir Drake

t first, I thought nothing would happen.

Then, as I was turning to go back toward the room I'd awakened in, the doors glided open, and a sleek, middle-aged man with dark hair and darker eyes prowled forward. He wore nothing but a dressing gown, but rather than making me feel more comfortable in my nightgown, his state of undress made me even more aware of my own inappropriate attire.

"Rilla, how good it is to see you up and about," he purred.

I shivered at the possessive way the man said my name. How did he know it anyway?

"We're sorry to bother you, sir," White girl said, "but Rilla has just remembered that the dragon, the one who destroyed her family? That dragon…" Her voice faded away as Sir Drake fixed her with a dark stare.

The man continued to stare at her until she shrank in on herself. "I'm so sorry. I'm sure you know all about it and have it well under control already. I should not have interrupted."

"No, you should not have," Sir Drake said.

I put an arm around the girl's shoulders. "She was understandably frightened by the thought of a dragon coming here, sir, though I can't imagine what she thought you'd be able to do about it."

The man turned slowly toward me. I thought I caught a glint of an oddly familiar dark stare, and then a black wall covered with golden chains dropped down between the man and me. The gold chains spread all around me. The palace and the girl at my side disappeared.

In another moment, even the cage was gone. I stood in a windy mountain dell, wrapped in the coils of a black dragon.

"What happened?" I asked.

I encountered chains I cannot break through without destroying your mind.

So, he'd seen the golden chains, too.

You shouldn't have been able to see them.

I shrugged. "I thought you needed to know what Sir Drake plots against you."

Not at that cost!

The dragon dropped away from me and sat just outside the mouth of his cave. I missed his warmth.

He chuckled, a sound warmer and less frightening than the dragon laughter in my memories.

"You're not the dragon who destroyed my farm," I blurted out.

No.

"But then…. I don't understand. I came here willingly. I'm sure I did. I can't remember why, but…. I'd know if I was here against my will, wouldn't I?"

I believe you would.

"I thought so. Still, I can't imagine agreeing to any such thing. Not unless…"

Unless?

"Unless I expected that doing so would lead to the capture and destruction of the dragon who killed my family."

Ah. You are bait in a trap.

"You're not that dragon!"

Sir Drake cannot afford to destroy the right dragon.

"Why…" Unless the crown really was in league with the dragon that destroyed my farm. White-hot fury flared inside me. Why should I feel so betrayed, though? I knew Sir Drake was cruel. "Why should he humor me, though? Why try to destroy you?"

He must *appear to be doing something about dragons to maintain his position, I suspect. And if you also are silenced in the process, you won't be able to tell anyone that he killed the wrong dragon. Besides, I am growing stronger. I suspect I'll be strong enough soon to escape the collar he fitted me with.*

I glanced at the gleam of gold on his neck. "Sir Drake gave you that? What does it do?"

Keeps me from taking a full bite, among other things.

Yes, I suppose that tiny loop would prevent him from eating people or cows whole the way the purple dragon at my farm had. "What other things?"

Using my full magic, changing form…

"Dragons can change form?"

The dragon laughed. It wasn't a happy sound.

"Sorry. I didn't mean to offend you."

You didn't.

I shivered, more from the cold than from the growl in his tone. The emerald eyes turned back toward me, he darted forward, and a claw shot out. Before I could be afraid, it pierced the rock above me, and my hands fell, the manacles around my wrists each trailing a small length of smoking chain. My jaw dropped open. "Thank you," I said, my voice shaking.

You're welcome. You should get inside before you freeze.

"Oh, but…" I glanced at the dark cave opening behind him. How did the giant beast in front of me fit in there?

Where the shoulders go, the rest of me can follow.

Like a rat.

Or a snake.

I shivered again.

Come. If an assault is coming, I can defend both you and myself better within. He turned and disappeared into the mouth of the cave.

I couldn't believe he'd left me unshackled out on the mountain. Nothing was forcing me to follow.

Except the cold, of course. Undoubtedly, the cave would be sheltered, perhaps even comfortable.

It is, very.

Hmm. I wondered if a dragon's idea of comfortable would be anything like my own.

Come and see.

"So, you can eat me in comfort?"

I have no intention of eating you, little one.

He didn't want to eat me? Then what did he want me to follow him for?

You were given to me, little one. You're my treasure now, and I must protect you. I can do that better from in here.

I took three steps closer to the mouth of the cave. "That other dragon said he'd keep me, too, but I'm not made of gold or jewels."

No, you are far more precious—a woman who can stand and speak her mind in the presence of a dragon. And you're beautiful as well.

I closed the distance to the cave mouth. The opening was low enough, I'd need to duck my head to enter. "Why would you even notice a human girl's looks?"

Why wouldn't I? There are no dragon girls, you know.

I shook my head and entered the cave.

"No dragon girls?" I'd never heard that before. It didn't make sense anyway. I'm sure I'd heard of dragon eggs and dragon hatchlings. Surely, it wasn't possible for a male anything to lay eggs.

The dragon chuckled, and in the darkness ahead of me, a sinuous, deeper darkness wavered. *Male dragons certainly don't lay eggs. Now come in a bit farther, and I'll shut the door.*

Shut the door? The cave mouth had no door that I could see. Still, I stumbled forward several more steps, running one hand along the right-hand wall and holding the other in front of me to make sure I didn't run into anything.

Behind me, rock rumbled and fell, completely blocking the cave entrance. The variegated darkness around me merged into a deep inky blackness. My heart sped, and I gulped. I was trapped in this mountain with the dragon, now.

CHAPTER FOUR

Dragon Mark

on't worry; just follow, the dragon thought into my mind.

"Follow what?" Even as I said it, a long trail of light appeared ahead of me. At first, I wasn't sure what I was seeing. Then I realized that the top row of the dragon's scales glowed with a green light that matched his eyes. They threw out enough light that the cave around me, though dim, was now visible.

Let me know if I go too fast. The light moved rapidly through the cave, which reminded me of nothing so much as an earthy tunnel. I had to walk quickly to keep up, and I had to keep up, for the dragon wound through a veritable maze of tunnels and caverns, bypassing dozens of openings in the cave walls only to turn suddenly into one that had no markings I could see. He did this again and again, never slowing, not even when the tunnels shrank, and I had to crawl. I wasn't sure how the dragon fit through at all.

I haven't eaten as well as I might have these last few years.

That collar kept him hungry, I supposed.

And humans keep infringing on my hunting grounds.

"Are you sure you're not infringing on their farms?"

My father marked our territory a thousand years ago, and we have maintained it perpetually ever since.

"Is your father the purple dragon?"

NO!

The dragon's light winked out. The earth around us trembled, and several small rocks fell. So, this was how it would end. I would die in darkness, wasting away, lost in the heart of the earth.

You are far too young to welcome death. The green light ahead of me winked back on.

"I'm not sure age has anything to do with it."

Perhaps you are right. For a long time after the purple dragon killed my father and mother, I, too, would have welcomed death.

The purple dragon had killed his parents, too? No wonder he got so angry when I suggested the monster was his father. Wait a moment. He said his mother and father? I thought he'd said earlier that dragons didn't have mothers.

I never said that. Dragon mothers are not dragons.

"Not dragons? Then what are they?"

Humans.

"Your mother was a human?"

Naturally.

"The purple dragon's mother was human?"

Yes, though it's doubtful he knew her. His clan encourages hatchlings to eat their mothers and sisters.

"But yours didn't?"

Of course not. That's disgusting. We honor dragon mothers and sisters.

"Do you have any sisters?"

I had two. They married humans and were lost when Sir Drake and your current king's father invaded their provinces.

"Sir Drake was alive in the time of the king's father?"

He is older than he looks.

He would have to be if what my dragon said was true. My dragon? When did I start thinking of the black dragon as mine? I didn't even know his name.

Vidar.

"What?"

My name is Vidar, and I like that you think of me as yours. I haven't belonged to anybody in a very long time.

He sounded so sad, I was almost tempted to forget he was a dragon and feel sorry for him.

I don't need your pity, but I require your companionship.

What if I didn't want to be his companion?

Then the coming years will be very hard for you.

"Coming YEARS?"

You are my sacrifice, are you not?

I supposed I was.

And you came voluntarily, yes?

I did. I mean, I had a strong suspicion Sir Drake had tricked me, but I had come of my own free, if uninformed, will.

Then you are stuck being my companion whether you desire it or not. Perhaps you will come to enjoy it in time.

I looked around me. The cave walls had become smooth and pearlescent, which was nicer than the dirty tunnels we'd traveled closer to the surface, but it was dim and dank, warmer than the mountainside, for sure, but hardly what I'd consider cozy. Would this be my home from now on? Already I missed fresh air, the feeling of wind on my face, the caress of the sun, and the pleasure of tending a plant or cradling a newborn lamb.

Once we've fully warmed you and found you sturdier clothes, I can take you to the farm. It isn't what it ought to be since I cannot work it when in this form, but it should satisfy your need for air and sunlight, and perhaps even sheep to cuddle if I can catch a few without harming them. I think there must be a way. Perhaps my father's books will say.

His father's books? Where would he keep books in a cave?

Vidar chuckled. *Come and see. We have reached Dragonhome at last.* He slipped through a tiny opening, and I crawled after him, stopping halfway through the aperture when I caught sight of the cavern beyond.

Vidar flew, brightly glowing, among shiny pillars, hills, and inverted cones, dancing and radiant in a world bigger and more wondrous than anything I had ever seen.

For long moments, I watched, astonished by the beauty and delight of my dragon.

I would never have guessed that such open, pearly forests existed below the ground. I crept forward out of the tunnel until I was fully in the room and could stand upright. Then I gently brushed a hand across the nearest luminous pillar. It was smooth and slightly wet.

Vidar swooped down and settled next to me. *Careful. The stalagmites and stalactites don't respond well to touch.*

I jerked my hand away. "I'm sorry. I didn't know."

Why should you? You've never been anywhere like this before.

I certainly hadn't. I smiled at him. He smiled back, rows of vicious teeth showing.

I backed up a step.

Sorry. He brought his lips down over his teeth in a rather painful-looking grin.

"Don't be. I shouldn't have reacted that way to your smile. I don't think you're going to hurt me."

I will not harm you, at least not on purpose. I swear it.

I smiled at him again. "Thank you."

I lifted a hand to touch the side of his face, and the bit of chain that still dragged from the manacle on my wrist nearly hit Vidar's neck. "I'm so sorry. I've been carrying these so long, I'd forgotten about them."

It is I who should be sorry. You should never have had to drag such cumbersome jewelry. Hold your hands out, palm up, and keep them very still.

I did as he said but couldn't help worrying as his claw crept closer.

I only touch the locks to direct my magic. I shall do no physical damage to you. I shall not even hurt the metal this time.

The tip of one claw touched on the keyhole of the manacle around my right wrist. Bright green light flashed, and the manacle dropped away. Then Vidar repeated the procedure with the second manacle.

"Thank you again."

Come. The human part of Dragonhome is this way. Vidar picked a path through the pillars and up and over several small rises. I'd known this cavern was big when I saw Vidar flying in it, but I hadn't realized it would take more than an hour to walk across. By the time we reached the far wall, I was footsore and hungry.

Here, a round gold disk, slightly wider than me, hung. Its center stood even with my waist.

It is a door.

Really? I couldn't see any handle.

It opens by magic. Place your hand in the center.

I did so, but nothing happened.

I forgot. I must officially claim you.

"How do you do that?"

I mark you as mine. Turn to face me and hold still, please.

"Will this hurt?" I slowly turned to face him.

I hope not. I promised I would not hurt you.

"But you don't know?"

I have never done it before, and naturally, I was not there when my father marked my mother.

His father marked his mother? Was Vidar claiming me as his wife?

Not just yet. This is merely a mark claiming you as part of my protectorate.

Ah, so I was a slave.

There are dragons who regard their protectees as such, but I think of it as more like family.

"Your marking me makes me part of your family?"

Yes.

I guessed that was all right. Better than being his wife or his slave, for sure, though I noticed Vidar hadn't ruled the former out. He'd only said he wouldn't claim me as his wife yet.

I want a willing wife, so I can wait until you are ready.

I doubted I'd ever be ready to be the wife of a dragon.

~ 21 ~

I hope I can change your mind about that, but do not worry about it now. Just hold still.

I did, and Vidar pointed one claw at a point just below my left collarbone. He moved the claw closer deliberately, as if he meant to stab me extraordinarily slowly.

I closed my eyes just before the claw touched, and braced myself for pain.

None came. Instead, I felt an uncomfortably hot pressure that spread from the touch going outward until my whole body flushed with warmth. Then the pressure pulled away. I opened my eyes and looked down. Where the claw had touched me, I could see a mark like a golden sun.

Apparently, I now belonged to a dragon.

CHAPTER FIVE

Dragonhome

"I t's beautiful," I said, still staring at the mark.

Thank you. Now try the door again.

I turned back to the golden disk and placed my hand in the center. This time, the metal beneath my palm warmed, and the disk swung up and to the right, as if on a peg placed near its upper right. In the place where the golden circle had been, a tunnel now yawned.

There should be a torch on either side of the door once you get through the entrance tunnel.

"How do I light it?"

Touch the base.

I scrambled into the tunnel as best I could with my voluminous skirts and crawled forward into the darkness. After covering about the length of the main part of my family's cabin—I swallowed a lump in my throat as I remembered my family's cabin no longer existed—the ground in front of me fell away. I backed up a bit into the tube, so as not to fall off the ledge. Leaning on my left hand, I probed the darkness with my right, finding nothing ahead of me, but a flat surface below and to either side.

That's the wall. Feel to your right.

I did so, and my hand caught on a thick pole. When I touched it, light sprang forth, glowing yellowish orange.

It illuminated a large room with flagstone floors and giant fireplaces at each end. In front of the one to my right, a huge bearskin rug warmed the floor, flanked by two rocking chairs. Next to one of them sat a knitting basket with black, brown, and white yarns and an unfinished sweater on top. The fireplace to the left had a mantel full of shiny copper pots and pans above it, and above that hung ladles, spoons, a bread board, and a rolling pin. The stone walls on either side of the fireplace held four cast-iron doors.

Four ovens?

Raising young dragons takes a lot of provender. There should be a step to help you into the room.

I looked directly below me and saw he was right. A wide stone step halved the distance between my tunnel floor and the floor of the room. The step was far enough down that crawling onto it wouldn't be graceful, but I could do it without hurting myself.

My mother always used to go through the tunnel backwards, but I wasn't sure that was best for you.

No. It was definitely better to go forward the first time, even if it meant a clumsy tumble on my arrival. At least this way, I could see what I was getting into. Besides, how would someone even get into the tube backwards?

She would lean on one of us.

Of course, she would. Well, good for her. There wasn't anyone for me to lean on here.

I haven't been able to fit in the human part of Dragonhome in my dragon form since I was a hatchling.

"So, you haven't been in here since you were a child?"

Not in dragon form, so not since this accursed collar was forced upon my neck.

"You sound like you miss it."

I do.

I inched my way forward and made it into the room by using an awkward crawl. Once in, I stood and shook out my now filthy skirts. I wondered if the fine fabrics could even be washed.

We can look for instructions on that as well in my father's books, but for now, perhaps you should see if any of the food has survived.

Food? If no one had been in this place for years, nothing left would be edible, even if the rodents had left it alone.

Our human food is magically protected, and no rodent would dare come near Dragonhome.

I supposed the proximity of dragons would tend to frighten smaller creatures away. I moved toward the cooking fireplace. A sturdy wooden table, glossy with polish and unbelievably free of dust, stood a few feet from the hearth. I imagined it served as both a work surface and a table for eating. I rounded the table and looked into the ovens, but they were empty. A fire sprang up when I touched a round stone below the mantle; however, I couldn't understand how that worked or what was burning. There was no sign of food.

Try the pantry.

"The pantry?"

On the right-hand wall as you face the kitchen fireplace, there are three small doors. The leftmost one is the pantry.

I swung to the right and saw the doors he must have meant, glad they were regular rectangles and not circles. Like the door to the house, they had no knobs.

Touch the center.

I was guessing that. I pressed my open palm against the door, and it swung outward. A torch like the ones at the door to the main room sat just inside the pantry opening on the left, and touching the torch filled the smaller room with a golden glow. I stepped inside and took stock of the heavily laden shelves around me. The wall nearest me held fruit of all sorts, firm and juicy, as if just plucked at peak ripeness from trees and vines. I picked up an apple and tentatively bit down. Tangy sweetness burst across my tongue, and the crisp flesh crunched as I munched the rest of it. How was this possible? By this time of year, even apples from this year's harvest would begin to soften and wrinkle, but the fruit I held in my hand had done neither.

No food in the pantry ever ages or spoils. If we wish to dry something, we must take it elsewhere.

Why would they wish to dry something if they could keep it in pristine shape forever?

I have a fondness for raisins.

"Oh." Sure enough, on one of the lower shelves of fruit, I found several crocks of raisins as well as ones holding dried apples, apricots, and peaches. "Do you want me to bring you some?"

That's very kind, but no. When a dragon, I eat only meat. Other foods give me indigestion, and I don't taste them properly anyway.

How sad. I looked for meat to take him, but that appeared to be the only type of food absent from the pantry. I found bread and flour, oil and yeast, vegetables in a dizzying array, herbs of all kinds, and a variety of cheeses, butters, and preserves, but no meat.

Dragons catch our own meals and also provide game for our protectees. I can hunt if you like.

"I think I'll be fine with what's here, but you should hunt if you're hungry."

I will be fine until I see you safely settled.

I wondered if I should be worried that his hovering felt more like concern than imprisonment to me.

I am concerned for you. I do not mean to trap you.

Funny how the reassurance heightened my concerns. But I chose to tamp down on them. Worrying added nothing of value to life.

At this moment, food was more important.

The food all looked so delicious, I wasn't sure what to choose, but when my stomach rumbled, I took what was easiest back out to the main room. I prepared bread with toasted cheese for myself and scarfed it down, not bothering to look for plates or utensils. The girls from the palace would have been appalled.

So would my mother, for that matter.

She would also insist I eat some vegetables, so in her memory, I ate two large carrots and another apple. Vidar's thoughts came as a hum of soft approval in my mind.

After eating, I felt thirsty, and Vidar directed me to the middle door, which held a second pantry, or perhaps it could be better called a wine cellar, though it was only half filled with wine racks. The other half held shelves filled with jugs of cider and milk. In the middle of the milk and cider half stood a sink with a spigot like that from a water pump above it. When I touched it, water flowed out into the basin and down through a hole in the center bottom. I looked under the basin and found a stone tube that led from the center of the basin into the wall. So, the water from the basin flowed into the wall?

All the wastewater in Dragonhome goes through the wall to a cleaning tank, and once clean, it flows into a nearby spring.

Amazing. I tapped the spigot, and it turned off. I tapped it again, and it turned on. "Is the water safe to drink?"

It is. You can find glasses behind the third door with all our tableware and cleaning supplies.

When I tried the third door, I found myself lost amongst a wealth of gold and crystal. On the lower shelves, I also found sturdy wooden cups and plates with a gloss that spoke as much of long, loving use as of fine workmanship. They reminded me of the ones we ate off at home. Those must have burnt with the house.

I picked up one of the cups and traced over the simple flower carvings that ran around the rim and up the handles. The wood felt silky under my fingers. Even Lark could not have made any finer.

Tears welled in my eyes, but I smiled as I brought the cup back to the drink pantry to fill it. The water was cool and mountain fresh. I drank three cupfuls before washing up and looking around for a place to rest.

The main nest is opposite the entrance door. You'll find my mother's clothes as well as the bathtub there.

Vidar's words in my mind shocked me since I hadn't heard him since going to look for the cup. I'd almost forgotten he was there. It was nice of him to give me a bit of privacy to think about my family.

The appearance of privacy, anyway. I have not yet discovered how to keep from hearing the humans in my vicinity. But enough of that. You seem tired, and the tub and bed both await.

I shuddered. Good as the water had been, I had no desire to bathe in anything so cold tonight, even if I had the energy to carry enough back to the nest, whatever that was.

Not to worry. The tub has its own spigots, both hot and cold.

This I had to see. I found the door to the main nest, as he called it. It turned out to be a room, both larger and warmer than the one with the two fireplaces. It had a lower ceiling, and a carpet covered most of the floor in a dizzying geometric pattern of green and black. In the center of the room sat an enormous mattress piled with emerald bedclothes and a multitude of cushions.

It looked so relaxing, so comfortable, I almost forgot about my search for the tub. I moved toward it as if in a dream, but as I neared the mattress, the filthy state of my clothes made me reluctant to touch the beautiful fabrics. Reminded of the promised bath and clean clothes, I turned about and saw a green screen embroidered with intricate, beautiful black dragons.

Behind it, I found a wide stone platform. Sunk into that sat a stone tub as big as the upper pond, the one that went dry some summers. It wasn't quite big enough to swim in, but nearly. The spigots filled it remarkably fast, considering its size. I adjusted the water until it was as hot as I could bear.

While the tub filled, I located a cedar trunk full of pretty, sturdy clothes a bit too large for me. The trunk also contained fluffy white towels and a bar of lavender-scented soap. I pulled these latter two items out along with a white flannel nightgown. With this bounty, I returned to the tub in time to turn off the water before it overflowed.

I couldn't remember ever feeling anything quite so lovely as that bath. I scrubbed off every bit of grime, making sure to rid myself of the mud that had found its way into my hair. Then, I drained the tub and started over with clean water, luxuriating in the sweet-smelling warmth. Only when the second bath had become so cold that I shivered did I pull the plug again. Quickly, I dried off and slipped into the softest nightgown I'd ever worn, even counting the one I remembered from the palace. That had felt slippery against my skin except where the lace scratched, but this caressed me.

The nightgown was only the beginning of comfort Soon, I sank into the feather pillows on the bed and snuggled into a nest of unparalleled softness.

I brushed a hand across what looked like a dragon in the carpet next to the mattress, and the light in the room dimmed to a glow like that of a fire across the room when it had burnt down to nothing but embers.

Since I left home the morning before the dragon attack, I'd never felt so safe.

Who would have guessed Dragonhome could make me feel that way?

CHAPTER SIX

Trapped

ragonhome did not feel nearly as safe when I discovered, after my rest, that I couldn't get out of it. Yes, there was ever-fresh food and a magical water pump, and even an amazing place to relieve oneself that flushed all the nastiness away with surprisingly little mess or fuss. Sure, there were places to work and places to play and places to sleep, and the most wonderful library I'd ever seen anywhere, even at the palace, but there was no way out. The door I'd come in wouldn't open in the other direction, no matter where I touched it, and I couldn't find any other doors that opened outward rather than into another part of the interior.

Even more strange, I hadn't heard the dragon's voice in my head since I'd awakened. Perhaps I'd imagined Vidar.

And my baths.

And the clothes I was wearing.

And the bread I kneaded beneath my palms.

Perhaps I was still chained to the side of the mountain dreaming a dragon-smoke inspired dream.

Or perhaps this was real, and Vidar had fallen into whatever trap Sir Drake had set for him. Perhaps he had died, leaving me trapped in Dragonhome until I died myself or went utterly mad.

What are you going on about?

"Vidar! You're not dead!"

Of course not, little one. I just went hunting for a spell.

"Hunting?"

I'm afraid I was hungry. I thought you would sleep until I returned.

Quite obviously, I hadn't. I'd had time to explore this whole place since waking. "Why couldn't I hear you?"

Mind speech travels farther than words of sound, but it cannot go more than a few miles.

"How far away were you?"

The other side of Burnt Pass. Game is scarce on the mountain at the moment.

"I suppose the deer don't like coming up this high while it is still winter."

Indeed. One of the reasons I look forward to my yearly cow.

Seriously? I was stuck in here, and he was harping on the cow again?

What do you mean, stuck in there?

"I can't get out."

The caverns are difficult to navigate on purpose. We do not want intruders to find their way to Dragonhome.

"If I'd made it into the cavern, I might or might not have been annoyed about that, but I think I'd understand. What I don't understand is being stuck behind this door."

How can you be stuck behind that door? Neither my mother nor any of my sisters ever had trouble opening it.

I crawled out to the entrance of the human part of Dragonhome and pressed my hand in the center of the golden circle. As before going this way, nothing happened.

That's impossible! Mother could always open it!

I believed him, Lord help me. Not even a dragon could fake the distress I heard in his thoughts. "What about the other members of your family?" I asked.

No, my sisters never had any trouble with it either, not even after they married.

"I meant the ones like me. Last night, when you marked me, you said you were making me like a member of your family."

A shadow flitted across my mind, the echo of a thought, but not the substance of it. So, that was what it felt like when Vidar wanted to keep something from me.

"You did make me a slave, didn't you?"

No! My family has no slaves. We never had any. Never! But...

The shadow slipped across my mind again.

"But the way you marked me—it's not the same as the way your father marked your mother, is it? You told me that, I think. You used the marking that's used for slaves, didn't you?"

I didn't know it would trap you in there. There is much I hadn't yet learned when—

"When Sir Drake forced that collar on you and kept you from your father's books."

Yes.

"So, you have made me a slave."

No! You are a member of my household. Not a slave. Never a slave.

"Then why am I trapped here?"

I don't know, but I can let you out.

A sound rang out, like a hammer hitting a gong, and the door swung up and open. I stared directly up Vidar's long snout into his emerald eyes.

I yelped at the suddenness of it. My heart beat a wild pattern in my ears.

I am sorry. I did not mean to startle you. I only wished to reassure you that you are not a captive.

"I'm not?"

Definitely not.

"You wouldn't mind if I wandered off?"

Of course, I would mind very much! You are my sacrifice, and I am already more than half bonded to you despite knowing the folly of it. All the same, I will not keep you here against your will if you choose to go.

The light on Vidar's scales flickered when he spoke, and I wondered if that indicated strong emotion.

You are far too perceptive for my peace of mind, little one.

"My name is Rilla, you know, and I'm not so little compared to other women."

I suppose not. It has been a long time since I saw any people, and my perspective may have changed. Would you like to go and see the farm now? I brought you three pair of sheep. I believe the females are pregnant.

He'd brought me sheep? "I thought you needed to consult your father's books for that."

It was easier than I expected. It turns out charming animals comes naturally to me.

I bet it did.

I have not tried to charm you!

I supposed, thinking back over our time together, I believed him. He was charming, but more in the way my brother Khan had been charming with the girls in the village than in some overpowering, magical way.

You find me charming?

I couldn't tell if he was pleased or offended. I smiled. "I would love to go to the farm with you, but perhaps I should finish the bread I'm baking first. Unless the sheep need us immediately?"

Finish your bread. They are fine where they are for now.

"You won't close the door on me?"

I shall keep it open anytime I am in the outer cavern.

Hmm. I considered my situation as I crawled backward into the main room. I would only be stuck in here when there wasn't a dragon guarding the entrance. That sounded better than being stuck in here always, but it didn't completely allay my fears about being trapped here, especially while he was out hunting. It was at least enough to ease my panic at being closed in for the moment.

We shall have to consider what to do about the times I am hunting. I do not like to leave you at the farm for long. That is how Sir Drake caught my mother.

"Sir Drake? I thought you said the purple dragon…" Sir Drake's oddly familiar black eyes flashed in my memory again. I felt on the verge of realizing something enormous, but the golden-chained black wall dropped again, this time with a punishing headache. I couldn't think, couldn't reason, couldn't even stand any longer. I fell to the stone floor, holding my head between my hands."

Sleep, my Rilla. We will speak no more of this.

❧

When I awoke, sometime later, in good health apart from some stiffness from sleeping on the stones in such an awkward position, the bread had puffed into a huge pillow, and I could not remember why I'd fallen asleep in such a strange place, in the middle of the day, too.

You triggered one of Sir Drake's mind traps, I'm afraid. It's probably best to avoid doing so again, at least until we can discover how to safely undo them.

"Let me guess. That will be in one of your father's books?"

Perhaps. He did not study mind magics overmuch.

Unusual for a dragon. Part of me wanted to rush immediately to the library to learn what I could, but the rest of me recalled something about the farm and sheep. The thought of fresh air had me rushing to bake my bread.

CHAPTER SEVEN

Flight

e had to fly to get to the farm. Like every other girl, I had sometimes imagined what it would be like to soar on the wind like an eagle, but, of course, I'd never imagined a person could really do it.

At first, I was hesitant to let Vidar pick me up, but when he explained that we could not reach the farm any other way, I decided the promise of fresh air was worth overcoming my fear of being clutched in a dragon claw.

In fact, the way Vidar held me bore little resemblance to the way the purple dragon had snatched up my family. First, we found and dragged out a large fur-lined sack that I stepped into and pulled up to my shoulders in front and over my head in back so that all of me but the front of my head was covered. I tugged on a drawstring at the mouth of the bag until the opening tightened into an O around my face.

There is a flap to cover your face if you like, but my mother and sisters always preferred to be able to see.

I found the flap he meant but left it alone. I suspected I, too, would wish to see where I was going.

Even though I expected it, I startled when Vidar grasped me around the waist. His grip was firm, but not uncomfortable.

My stomach swooped as we lurched into the air. I felt sure we were going to crash, but we didn't. Vidar pumped his wings, and we jerked upwards. With each flap, we first dropped and then shot further toward the cavern roof.

I was beginning to regret having agreed to fly (and had long since regretted eating breakfast that morning) when the flight evened out, and we soared, turning now and then, up tunnel after wide tunnel, always rising, until we drifted to a stop in a cavern half as big as the cavern part of Dragonhome. I hoped Vidar realized this was not outdoors.

Of course. We must walk the next bit. We wouldn't want just any dragon to be able to fly directly into Dragonhome.

I supposed not. I slipped out of the flying sack, and at Vidar's instruction, rolled it up, stuffed it into a small bag, and tied it to his foreleg. Then I followed him through a maze even more confusing than the one we'd navigated the day before. I'd think dragons were paranoid if it weren't for the awful fact that all these precautions hadn't been enough to save Vidar's family.

It wasn't always that way, or so my father used to say. Once, long ago, before his time, dragons lived at peace with each other and with other people. Back then, Dragonhome was the name for the city where most dragons dwelt. That is an evil place now, full of violence and slavery. They have changed the name to The City.

"Where is that?"

Far from here. Eastward, on the other side of the eastern mountains.

I shuddered. Even my small village had heard ugly tales of an evil country to the east. We called it Arkon, and no traders went that way. As far as I knew, there weren't even any roads.

Dragons do not need them.

True enough. I wondered what kept those eastern dragons away from us.

I do. I, and the magical wall my father built. The purple dragon is the only one who has come through, and that was through a trick, not strength. He would burst the wall wide if he could, but I have patched every hole he has made and soon will be strong enough to destroy him altogether.

The collar around Vidar's neck glowed for a moment and then faded. I believed him when he said he would soon be rid of it. I wondered what he meant by soon.

Vidar chuckled. *You ask good questions, my Rilla. I wish I knew for certain. This year, I think, or perhaps next.*

And then he would kill the purple dragon. The thought gladdened me as very little had recently.

My mother would be disappointed if she knew that revenge had become the only thing to gladden my heart.

Not the only thing, surely. You seemed glad enough in that bath last night.

"Vidar!"

Is it not true?

"You should not be paying attention when I bathe."

I cannot help it.

"Try harder!"

Vidar stopped in front of me.

"What is it?"

Time to fly again.

I realized we had reached another large cavern. "Oh." With nearly as much trepidation as before my first flight, I unstrapped the flight sack from Vidar's leg, opened it up, and climbed into it. This time, I didn't jump when Vidar gently gripped me, nor did I find the take-off as jerky. After one great flying leap upward, we soared into a tunnel that sloped downward at a steep angle for what felt like forever, until it leveled out and opened into a third giant cave.

It's all walking from here.

"All right," I said, though I wasn't sure how much more walking I could take.

It's not far now, but we can rest a while if you need to.

"No, no. I'm fine." I had to find a way to block Vidar from my mind when I wished to.

I don't know if you can. Human minds are rarely capable of such things, but perhaps you can do it. You have successfully resisted Sir Drake's mind magic, after all.

"That wall he locked my memory behind? It's still there, isn't it?" Even thinking about it made my head ache.

It is impressive that you can see it, but I speak more of your distaste for the man.

"He's unpleasant, and I don't like the way he looks at the other girls and me."

Nor do I, but few can resist Sir Drake's enchantments when he wishes to enthrall them.

"Perhaps he did not try to enthrall me."

When he wanted you for his wife? I doubt that.

I'd forgotten the bit of memory where the girls claimed I was Sir Drake's betrothed. Had I agreed to become a sacrifice to avoid that fate?

It wouldn't surprise me, but if you wish to see the farm today, perhaps it would be best not to try to remember. I do not wish you to have another headache you must sleep off.

I suspected Vidar was right, though my memory of headaches and sleep was fuzzy. I followed him through several more winding passages, each smaller than the last until I was crawling rather than walking, and Vidar crept on his belly, stretching himself thin like a snake, his wings plastered close against his sides like a second skin. Nearly there indeed!

CHAPTER EIGHT

Sheep

idar chuckled and moved a bit to the left. Light washed through the tunnel. I covered my eyes with one hand until I could adjust to it.

Once I could bear the light, I crept forward a few more feet and came out of the cave system into a surprisingly warm mountain dell, green with grass and leafy trees despite the season.

A small group of sheep grazed between the blackened stumps of what must once have been an orchard. When they caught wind of us, instead of bolting, as any reasonable sheep would, they ran toward Vidar, nuzzling him and playfully hitting their heads against his sides. With the curly-horned rams, their assault would have hurt a less armored creature, but Vidar seemed hardly to feel it. In fact, he gave the sheep the kind of indulgent stare my father used to give his dogs when they greeted him on his return from a trip to the village, and I revised my opinion of their actions. If anything could prevent a sheep from being on a dragon's supper menu, it was this.

Though I doubted it would work with the purple dragon.

Nay. That one would think it funny to slowly devour a creature that thought he loved it. I believe it is what he most often does with women. They never last long enough to bear him children—or at least none have since I have known him.

I shuddered.

Not that he wants children. He'd see them as competition.

I was strangely comforted to learn the purple dragon would not produce more monsters like itself. One was surely enough. "What shall we call them?"

What shall we call who?

"The sheep."

What is wrong with sheep?

I laughed. "That's what they are all together, but each one is its own as well. See how this one pushes the others about? Perhaps we should call him Tyrant. And this smallest one is Little Lady. And that one—I pointed at one of the other ewes who had bits of fern dangling from one side of her mouth—Fern, I think."

So, the dark ewe should be Blackie?

"Good idea. And the other ewe is Dancer."

The young ram, then, is Buster.

"You're getting it. Why did you bring two rams?"

I tried to find one for each ewe, but there weren't so many around.

"Sheep and cows are like deer. One male collects lots of females and usually chases the other males off. Haven't you noticed this before?"

Some dragons are like that, too, and I hate it. I won't have such behavior on my farm.

"How will you stop it?"

Vidar rested one foreclaw on Tyrant's head and the other on Buster's. Then he exhaled a puff of air that encircled all of us, dragon, human, and sheep. In the air floated a compulsion to be kind to all in the group. I wasn't sure how I knew this. I couldn't see it, couldn't smell it, couldn't touch it, but I knew, all the same, that a compulsion floated in the fog. I put my hand up, as if to block it, and the fog swirled around me but left a space a few inches from my skin.

Impressive. I have never seen a human so resist a dragon command before. Not even my sisters could do it.

"I don't like to be forced to do things."

I see that. Vidar chuckled. *I only included you in the group so that the sheep would recognize you also as family, and I didn't think you would mind being kind to them since having them here was your idea.*

"Oh." So, it was. I put down my hand and dropped my resistance. The fog crept back toward me, and slipped through my skin, into every part of me. As it infused me, I felt all my protective and nurturing resolves toward Vidar and the sheep strengthen while my tendency to distrust weakened.

Wait one moment. Did I really want my distrust of Vidar weakened? He was a dragon, powerful and deadly still. I'd only known him since yesterday, and though that was enough to prove he was no monster like the purple beast, it was hardly enough time to ensure he was fully trustworthy. Hadn't he misled me about the marking and left me trapped underground?

As if pulling a single thread in a weaving, I plucked the part of the compulsion that kept me from distrusting Vidar, separated it from the rest, and cast it from me.

Amazing. I wish I could kiss you.

I stared at Vidar's long scaly snout, horrified.

Don't worry. I won't do it. Not in this form, anyway, and not unless you welcome it.

That would be the day.

You never know. You might find my other form attractive.

"Why? What does your other form look like?"

I don't rightly know, to be honest. I was not yet mature when Sir Drake forced this collar on me.

"How old were you then?"

Twelve summers.

"And that was around the time the purple dragon attacked? You were still mostly a child, then. How did you survive? Did he let you go like he did me?"

Nay. The purple beast takes no pleasure in ravishing boys that I have ever heard of. He saves that torture for maidens, and so far as I know, he prefers them full-grown, or nearly so. Well-ripened, I think he calls it.

I shivered and looked down at my full chest and narrow waist. My sisters had often said my assets would catch men's eyes. A pity they also attracted dragons.

You are lovely, but your strength of mind is even more captivating than your body. I suspect you ensnared the purple monster the same way you are enthralling me—with the strength of your will. When the purple dragon attacked here, though, I escaped another way. While the beast fought my father, I used the time their battle provided to cast a powerful spell—one that still holds. Any damage that dragon does to me, he does equally to himself.

"You hoped he would destroy himself killing you."

He nearly did. Unfortunately, he chose to kill me slowly, wanting to draw out the torture with a victim too weak to threaten him. As soon as he began, of course, he discovered my spell. Amazingly, he could find no way to undo it.

"So, you are safe from him?"

He cannot kill me himself without losing his own life. He often sends others to do the work for him. So far, none have succeeded, but I stay vigilant.

I would, too. I did not like that purple dragon, and I had a nasty feeling the beast wasn't done with me. It almost made me want to scurry back underground.

I didn't mean to live that way, though, hiding from the sky, cowering in fear. For now, I would enjoy my time out in the open, getting to know the sheep and this farm.

The farm had clearly burned. Beside the burnt husks of trees in the orchard, soot stained the exterior of the stone buildings, and the ground itself looked blackened under its crop of weeds. "When you said you couldn't tend the farm as you ought, did you mean you couldn't tend it at all?"

The first spring, I tilled a field, but couldn't get into the granary for seed, nor into the treasury for gold to buy any from the men in Westmarket. When I thought about conducting business while in this form, and remembered I couldn't eat the produce anyway, I gave up the idea.

"Hmm. Do you remember the best time for planting? It should be winter still but doesn't feel like it is here."

We usually plant grain after the Harvest Celebrations have ended. We start tender vegetables in the greenhouse after the New Year. Mama would transplant them the first of spring.

That was a full six weeks ahead of my farm in the valley, but I could easily adjust. "Where was the seed?"

In there. Vidar pointed his right foreleg at the largest of the farm buildings, a block of gray stone twice as big as any of the barns on my farm. From where I stood, there did not appear to be any opening. As I walked around it, though, I found covered pens for sheep and cows that used the great block as their back wall. Coming around to the far side of the block, I found a golden disk the same size as the door to Dragonhome and patterned with the same carvings. I pressed my hand to its center, and it swung open. I wondered if this door, too, would trap me if it closed.

I will not close it. Vidar reassured me.

Nodding, I crawled through the opening. This entrance tunnel lasted only a few feet before ending at another round golden door, which also swung open at my touch.

Unlike in Dragonhome, no torch met my exploring fingers.

Touch the wall under the tunnel to obtain light.

I reached downward, and the space in front of me flooded with light, nearly as bright as the world outside.

I wasn't sure what to expect. At my family farm, the barns were dim and warm and full of the pungent aroma of animals. This place held little resemblance to that except in the smell of fresh hay, and the familiar shapes of spades and hoes.

I found the seed bags in a corner opposite the door. Though the varieties were not the kinds I knew, I

recognized seeds for all kinds of vegetables and herbs—
melons, squashes, eggplant, beans, peas, peppers, lettuce,
cabbage, asparagus, rhubarb, parsley, fennel, coriander,
oregano…I dipped my fingers into each bag and let the
wealth slide over my fingers. If these could still sprout,
they'd fill a vegetable garden bigger than the one at home.

The feel of tiny seeds slipping over my fingers put
me in mind of steamy mornings spent in the greenhouse
with my mother and sisters, starting rows of seeds in old
rags. A tear slipped down my cheek, and then another
followed, and another, until I crouched on the floor next to
the seed bags, sobbing, my head cradled in my arms.

CHAPTER NINE

Rubble

 *illa—my little one—Rilla—What is wrong?*

Vidar's voice in my head sounded so frantic, it pulled me from my cry. I wiped my face on my sleeves and wished for a handkerchief. I'd make sure to put one in my dress pocket the next time I was back at Dragonhome to change. "I am fine," I said. "You can read my mind—surely you knew that."

You had no thoughts, only pain.

"I was thinking of my family."

Oh, then I am sorry to have interrupted you. You need your tears.

Perhaps he was right, but I couldn't go back to them now. My memories had reminded me of more than the disaster. "You said something about a greenhouse, but I don't remember seeing one."

We used to have a beautiful greenhouse, but it will take some work to repair. We can start on that once you've checked the grain.

"I didn't see any grain."

In the stone barrels.

Stone barrels? I'd never heard of such a thing, but once Vidar mentioned them, I saw what he meant. Casks of seamless stone lined the wall to my right. Their tops reached my shoulder, and I wondered how I would look into them, assuming I could lift the covers.

There should be a ladder.

I found a sturdy wooden stepladder on a wall of tools. It was heavy, but not too heavy for me to carry. From its second step, I could see the tops of the stone barrels. Their covers were carved in the same manner as the Dragonhome and barn doors. I placed my hand palm down in the center and nearly fell off the ladder when I had to jerk backwards to avoid the cover swinging towards me.

Only after I was sure it had stopped completely did I move back close enough to the barrels to peer inside. The seeds looked like wheat berries but were redder than any I had ever seen.

Dragonwheat, Vidar planted in my brain. *The magic of the casks should have kept them good, even if their own magic did not.*

Like the food in the pantry in Dragonhome. But Dragonwheat? I'd heard tales of it but had thought they were myths.

Not at all.

If all the casks contained seeds like this, then Vidar had more wealth in this barn than I'd ever before seen in my life.

Vidar chuckled. *It will be worth even more if we can plant it, but most of the fields are in even worse shape than the greenhouse. I don't know if we can ready them in time for a crop this season.*

He probably knew best. I'd never paid much attention to raising wheat. Papa and the boys did that.

We will attend to the greenhouse, so you can work with the plants you are most familiar with. Then we will attend to the fields and orchards.

That sounded reasonable enough.

Bring the wheelbarrow and black gloves.

I found the items he'd mentioned, emerged from the stone shed, and followed Vidar down a path between wide fields of weeds until we reached a ruinous mass of rubble and broken glass. Was that the greenhouse?

Yes. It was beautiful once, but it didn't make sense to fix it before now. I cannot fit inside it when I'm in this form.

Fix it? I wasn't even sure we'd be able to clear it out of the way so we could start fresh.

What kind of dragon would I be if I could not move stone?

I'd never heard of dragons moving stone—only of them marauding, burning, and killing. But they obviously tunneled in mountains, so it made sense that they could. "I'm sorry…it's just…where do we even start?"

I shall move the larger stones while you pick up the smaller. We shall deal with the glass last of all. Vidar picked up a boulder from the top of the pile of rubble and hop-flew it to the nearest field. Then he came back for a second, which he sat beside the first.

I chose a spot far from the center where he was working and gathered smaller stones that were still big enough that I needed to lift them with two hands. Before I'd filled my wheelbarrow halfway, Vidar had a neat stack of boulders piled in the nearby field, and the rubble showed a noticeable dent. I sped up my own cleanup efforts.

Even with dragon speed and strength, the mound of rubble grew smaller only slowly. Sweat pooled between my breasts, and my shoulders ached. Rarely had I worked so hard. By the time the sun dropped below the western peaks, every inch of me cried out for rest, and I could barely stand upright.

Vidar encouraged me to wash in a bitingly cold stream and to eat some bread and cheese from the satchel I'd packed that morning. Then I put my traveling bag down on one of the fields, climbed into it, and fell almost instantly asleep.

When I awoke in the pale light of dawn, I found Vidar curled about me, so that I lay within a circular wall of black dragon scales. My heart sped up, but before I could get properly frightened, the wall around me shifted, leaving a way out.

I wandered out to the stream, where the sheep had gathered. They greeted me as they had greeted Vidar yesterday, and I couldn't help laughing as they begged to be petted and gamboled like lambs. Beautiful little beasts. I hugged Little Lady, and then asked the herd to give me some privacy, so I could relieve myself. Addressing them so only made them nudge me all the more. Silly creatures. I adored them, but that didn't mean I wanted them to witness my morning ablutions.

Send them to me.

Vidar was up?

Dragons don't sleep the way you do. We rest only half our minds at a time while the other half stays awake to keep watch.

That accounted for the legends about how difficult it was to catch a dragon napping. "Go see Vidar," I cooed at the sheep.

Blackie perked up her ears. Dancer trotted in a circle. Tyrant butted my shoulder.

"Silly sheep," I said.

They all gazed at me with wide, adoring eyes. I shook my head. It didn't look like they were going anywhere without me this morning. "Come along, then." I led them back toward Vidar. They followed in a skipping, leaping bunch, rubbing and bumping up against each other almost as much as they nudged me. I was glad to pen them between Vidar's coils. Why had I wanted sheep again?

You love them.

I supposed I did, but I couldn't stay to talk about it. I was nearly bursting. Vidar laughed as I ran back toward the stream.

When I returned after relieving myself and splashing water on my face, I found Vidar hard at work on the rubble pile and the sheep grazing nearby. I supposed I should get to work as well, but my muscles ached more than any country girl's had a right to after a day of honest labor. How long had I been at the palace, and what had I been doing there?

There is no need to wear yourself out.

"Thank you, but I'd rather work with you than watch you labor alone."

At least eat something before you begin.

"Have you eaten yet?"

I ate yesterday. In my dragon form, I only eat about once a week. Less often if the meal is a very large one.

"Like the cow you were supposed to get."

I never ate the cows. They were always traps.

"Poisoned?"

Some of them. Some were rigged to magically explode when I touched them. Some were meant as distractions from ambushes. That's what I expected when I saw you.

"Do you still expect it?"

No. I think Sir Drake has something far more complicated than a simple ambush up his sleeve.

I wished I could remember more. Then, perhaps, I could help Vidar.

If you want to help me, eat your breakfast. Without sustenance, you'll hardly be able to lift pebbles for long.

I laughed and found the satchel of food. As I munched the day-old bread, I thought over all Vidar had told me. "If you didn't want the cow for food, why did you ask so much about it when we first met?" I asked Vidar as he levered another giant stone loose from the mound of rubble.

I was so flummoxed by finding you there. Sir Drake always brings a cow on New Year's Day, so I was hiding out, waiting to spring the trap—and then, for the first time ever, there was no cow. I was expecting the creature to wander out of a hidden crevasse or appear from out of a magic mist. But there was no cow.

"Only me."

Only you. You are quite enough.

"I'm afraid I've been a lot of trouble for you."

Vidar let the stone he was lifting roll back onto the pile and tipped his head to one side. *It is good to have someone worth troubling about.*

I met his gaze. He was right.

I, too, felt better for having someone and something to care for, and I'd only lost my family a few months ago, if it was harvest then and New Year now. I nodded at Vidar, and he bared his teeth in what might have been meant as a smile.

I smiled back, wondering how long Vidar had been alone, without either animal or person for company.

It was a wonder he hadn't gone insane.

He hadn't, had he?

CHAPTER TEN

Glass

y late afternoon, Vidar and I had cleared all the stones away and gathered the broken glass into a giant black cauldron Vidar had dragged out of one of the openings that pocked the mountainsides around us.

"What are we going to do with that?" I asked.

Repair the glass. Let me get the rest of my tools, and I'll show you.

Vidar ducked back into another crack in the mountain face and returned with a sturdy metal table. The third time he disappeared into the mountain, he reappeared with a couple of long metal pipes, two dense wooden bowls, and something that looked like a very large wooden hoe.

Stand well back. If you move to that small hillock, you should be able to see everything.

I did as he suggested, sitting atop a hill where I could see Vidar, the cauldron full of glass shards, and the odd collection of instruments that Vidar laid carefully in a row. Then he took in a long deep breath and blew a steady stream of fire at the cauldron. At first, little happened, but soon the glass within glowed orange and then red. At this point, Vidar took one of the long tubes and dipped it into the glowing glass, removing a ball of the reddened stuff, which he rounded into a circle in one of the wooden bowls while still streaming fire at the cauldron.

He'd been blowing fire for more than five minutes now, and I wondered if he'd soon need to take a breath, but he didn't seem to. Perhaps he was breathing through his nose as he flamed out of his mouth. However it worked, the flames didn't stop as he added more glass to his ball and shaped it in the larger bowl. Then he took a second pipe and thrust it through the first one, for what purpose, I could not discern, for he removed the smaller pipe almost immediately. Then he stopped shooting flame but brought his mouth to the end of the pipe opposite the glowing glass ball. Then he blew, twirling the pole between his foreclaws as he rose in the air.

The ball of glass grew like a soap bubble, and then, as Vidar swung it in addition to blowing and turning, it lengthened. When it was as long as my arm and back to looking more colorless than red, Vidar sank back to earth, rested the elongated glass on the table, and scored a straight line from one end of the bubble to the other. Then he pinched each end with his claws until the ends fell away, and Vidar could drop them back into the cauldron. After setting the pipe on the ground, Vidar blew flames over the tube he'd created. When it glowed faintly orange again, he inserted his claws into the line he'd scored at the top and pried the tube apart, flattening the cylinder until it lay upon the table. There, he used the hoe-looking thing to smooth it until it looked like the biggest, thinnest pane of glass I'd ever seen.

"Is it finished?"

Nearly. I need to keep it warm, so it cools down slowly and doesn't crack. Vidar blew a river of fire over the glass, slowly decreasing the amount of flame until it was a trickle and then nothing but a cloud of steam. When the steam had fully cleared, he lifted the giant glass, set it upright in one of the pens that leaned against the barn, and repeated the whole procedure. He did it again and again, all that day and for two days more.

It was fascinating watching him work, but after a while, my idleness bothered me, so I explored the farm, finding more barns and a sleeping hut with spare clothes and a supply of magically preserved food, smaller than Dragonhome's, but plenty for several weeks.

The fresh clothes inspired me to wash the ones I was wearing and bathe while I was at it, not that I lingered long—the stream was mountain cold even if the basin where the farm sat was warm.

While I shivered my way into the clean clothes, I noticed rushes at the water's edge. That would be perfect for baskets. It would be pleasant to have something to do while Vidar blew glass. I whistled as I went for a knife. Mother would be appalled if she could hear me, but Khan would be proud. He had taught me to whistle and would sometimes harmonize with me when we worked harvests together.

At that memory, the whistle fell from my lips, but at least this time, when I cried, I had a handkerchief to sniffle into.

When I'd had my good cry, I gathered my rushes and returned with a bucket of water to the hilltop where I could watch Vidar. I ate a light lunch and then started on a large basket to use at harvest time. It was slow going. Vidar had finished four panes of glass before I completed the bottom spiral and started up the sides, but he didn't have to fend off inquisitive sheep. In fact, it seemed as if he'd set some invisible fence around his workspace, for the sheep circled him but never crossed a line about two dragon lengths from where he was working.

I wished I could convince the sheep to stay away from me. I waved Buster away from my rushes and settled back into my weaving, but I couldn't help stopping whenever Vidar got to the part where he swung the glass bubble to lengthen it. As the swinging ball of molten glass swayed, so did I, rocking right and then left, enthralled.

Whenever Vidar then grabbed the glass in his claw, I winced, though Vidar showed no sign of discomfort. Perhaps creatures who could spew fire were immune to heat. I wished I were immune to heat. More importantly, I wished my family had been.

But not even Vidar's father and brothers had survived the purple dragon's attack, so maybe dragon skin wasn't completely impenetrable.

I returned to my work.

By the next evening, I had finished my basket, and Vidar said he'd finished all the glass we needed. I sat, leaning against his side, to eat my supper, while the sheep grazed nearby. The sunset gleamed orange and gold over the tops of the peaks, and I relaxed.

The next morning, after I woke and ate, I found Vidar on the site of the greenhouse, stomping and snorting. I ran towards him. "Vidar, what's wrong?"

He stopped. *Nothing. I'm setting the foundation.*

He was what? That wasn't how people made foundations.

Dragons do it this way. Come look.

I came closer and discovered that the ground beneath his feet had become a large, perfectly flat stone. I knelt down and touched it. It was as cool and smooth as my mother's rolling pin. I wondered if that had survived the fire, not that I wanted to sift through the ashes of my old home to find out.

It is not fun to explore wreckage, but sometimes it helps. If ever you wish to, I will help you.

That was sweet of him. I clutched at my handkerchief but decided I'd rather not have a crying jag this morning. There was work to be done. "Well, this looks beautiful. What's next? How do we build this? I've never worked with stones." Or at least not ones this size. Khan, Lark, and I had once built an oven in a clearing in the woods. We'd stacked smooth rocks and mortared the chinks with clay from the riverbank.

The stone stacking is the same, but I've never used mortar.

"How do you hold the stones together?"

Heat and magic.

"I thought your collar kept you from doing magic."

Not completely. And whenever I exercise my magic, the collar cracks a bit.

"Really?"

Look.

Vidar lowered his head so near me that he was close enough I could reach out and touch his neck. The collar gleamed against his black scales, but up close, I could see myriad tiny black cracks running through the gold. I traced one of them. This happened when Vidar used magic? What would happen if he used lots of magic? Would the cracks widen enough that Vidar could free himself of this thing?

Let's find out.

Setting the stones in place was more a matter of strength than anything else. Once he'd laid out a large rectangle around the outer edges of his smooth foundation stone, Vidar had me help him fill the cracks between the giant stones with smaller ones. Then I stood well back while he blew flame at one of the joins. He stared intently at the crack, and his flame turned as emerald as his eyes. The stone under the flame smoothed and sealed together, growing until the two boulders looked like one, perfectly smooth, rock.

The stream of fire stopped. *There. I must rest a minute. Can you fill the next crack?*

Vidar slumped to the ground as if his bones had suddenly become liquid.

"Vidar!"

I'll be fine after a break. He winked the eye nearest me.

I hoped so. It took much longer to fill the next crack between two large stones by myself than it took when Vidar helped, but if he needed rest, he needed rest. In fact, if this was too much for him, perhaps we didn't need a greenhouse.

The food stores won't last forever. And my farm has lain fallow too long. Much, much too long. I should have repaired this years ago, but I had so little reason to. Now, with you here, I have reason to work again.

"You haven't worked the farm since your parents died?"

Vidar's eyes lowered, and his scales seemed to ripple. What did that mean?

I'm embarrassed. I know I should have fixed up the farm years ago.

"Well, at least you're doing it now."

One wheelbarrow full was enough for this crack. While I went for a new supply of small stones, Vidar did his green fire trick again. This time his slump seemed less boneless. Odd. When I repeated difficult work, I got more tired, not less. I filled a third seam as he rested, and again went to fetch more stones while Vidar used his magic on the section I'd just filled.

When I returned the next time, I could see the cracks in Vidar's collar even from halfway along the new greenhouse wall. I smiled. That thing was going to break, and then Vidar would be free.

That was a good thing, right?

Don't worry. I understand. An unrestrained dragon is a terrifying thing.

"How will it change you?"

I'll be able to use my father's spell books and learn more complicated and powerful magic. I'll be able to change form.

"But will it change who you are—what you're like?"

I hope not, but who can say?

I hoped not, too. I rather liked the Vidar I'd met, though I'd been with him for less than a week. He was thoughtful and wise, and he worked incredibly hard.

I'm blushing again.

"That thing with your scales was a blush?"

Of course. What did you think it was?

I shrugged. "When I blush, I usually turn red."

Scales don't change color.

Apparently not. I focused on my work.

By noon, we'd laid one level of stone. After lunch, Vidar used blue as well as green fire to shape the next stone into a window rather than a solid block. He looked as tired after that first window as he had after the first solid seam, but after two or three of them, his rests became shorter. I filled gaps in the stone faster and faster to keep up with him.

By the time evening fell, I was more than ready for a break. I bathed in the freezing river, swallowed a bit of supper, and collapsed in the bunkhouse. When I awoke, Vidar had long been hard at work. I found him circling the remaining rubble, which he had organized into what looked like an extraordinarily heavy roof of solid rock for the greenhouse.

"How did you do this without making any noise?"

I made lots of noise. I don't know how you slept through it.

I shook my head. My muscles ached, but I felt extraordinarily well rested. I suspected I hadn't slept this well in months, perhaps not since the attack on my farm.

It wouldn't surprise me. Grief can do terrible things to one's ability to sleep.

I smiled at Vidar. "Then why aren't I having any difficulty now?"

You're working too hard. Though you won't be today. I think the roof is ready for me. Make sure you and the sheep are a good distance away.

I gathered our six woolly friends and led them into a nearby pen. Vidar spouted green and blue flames, transforming the pile of rocks into a lattice of thick, stone, window frames. After every few frames, he took a break, but these were shorter than yesterday's.

To keep myself busy, I petted the sheep, and when they got busy foraging in the winter-browned fields, I collected more rushes and started a new basket—a smaller one, for picnics, this time.

By the time I'd finished, Vidar had completely transformed his pile of rocks. "Now what?" I asked him.

I'll set it atop the greenhouse walls and seal it on.

"Vidar, even without all the windows, that roof must weigh more than most houses. It's stone."

It won't be a problem. There's no magic in this, Rilla, just brute strength. He leapt atop his roof and grabbed each corner with a claw. Then he spread his wings and flapped a few times. Great gusts of wind slapped against me, but the roof stayed planted on the ground. Vidar flapped faster, and I ducked my head. With a great creak, I assumed of Vidar's bones, Vidar and the roof rose. At first only waist high, but then up into the sky, and over to the greenhouse, where Vidar hovered, slowly turning, until the roof aligned perfectly with the walls beneath it. Then slowly, slowly, he lowered it. When it rested fully on the walls, he leapt back off.

See, nothing to it.

"Then why are your sides heaving like you're a horse who has galloped into a lather?"

Vidar grimaced in what I suspected was meant to be a smile. *Almost nothing to it. When I get my breath back, I'll seal it on, and we can put the glass in tomorrow.* He suited his actions to his words, and by the time I sat down with him to eat my supper, he had finished.

That night I slept restlessly, and I woke before the sun had risen. Maybe Vidar was right about hard work being the cure for insomnia. While he magically installed the windows, he'd made in the openings in the greenhouse frame, I found a collection of stone pots in the barn and filled them with rich black earth from a pile tucked back against the mountain. From the smell and feel, it would make excellent seed starter. This must have once been a compost heap.

Something like that.

"What do you mean?"

I think you've found the old collection point for dragon droppings. I haven't used that one since my father was ambushed there.

I'd found a dragon outhouse? I dropped the pot I was filling.

Vidar laughed. *If it helps, dragon droppings make extraordinarily good fertilizer.*

I shivered.

Oh, come on. Surely, you've grown things in cow patties.

Of course, I had. But the cows never talked to me.

Vidar laughed again. *If you'd rather, the real compost pile is in the fourth pen on the western side of the main barn.*

I hauled all the pots back to the barn and found the heap Vidar had recommended. It also was a rich black loam, though not, I suspected, as rich as the last pile.

No, it wouldn't be. Are you sure you don't want to use the dragon droppings?

I was sure. The compost was plenty rich enough and didn't make me want to spend an hour washing my hands.

Before the sun set that evening, Vidar had completed the biggest, most beautiful greenhouse I'd ever seen. I moved my pots in, setting them on window ledges and the floor in readiness for planting tomorrow.

The day after tomorrow, Vidar said into my mind. *Tomorrow we must return you to Dragonhome, so I can go hunting.*

No. Absolutely not. I refused to be trapped in that place beneath the earth again.

CHAPTER ELEVEN

Argument

"Why can't I stay here?"

I have done my best to restore the protections of the farm, but the purple dragon attacked here once and can do so again. I cannot help but leave the sheep, but I will not risk you.

It sounded sweet but felt confining. I tapped the brand on my collarbone.

Please, Rilla. I don't know if I could survive losing you.

He'd survived the loss of his whole family, but thought he might not survive losing me? Ridiculous.

When a dragon bonds to a woman, it is different than the bond between family members.

"Are you saying you've bonded to me?" An unreasoning panic took hold of me.

Vidar didn't answer. What did that mean?

If you let him trap you in the hill, you'll belong to him forever.

Who was that? Not Vidar. Vidar never sounded so sinister or threatening.

Someone else is talking to you? This time it was Vidar.

"Yes, the way you speak to me, but not the same. Is he here? You said you can't speak to me that way unless you're nearby!"

Vidar growled. *Get in the barn. Why can't I sense him?*

Vidar's panic propelled me forward, and I ran for the stone structure. A glimpse of purple flashed in the corner of my eyes as I ducked inside. Flames shot out behind me. Then I was left in cool darkness. Outside, I heard roars and dragon screams. Then came an enormous crash and a great rumble. After that, there was silence.

Nothing.

"Vidar? Vidar! Are you all right?"

The silent darkness swallowed my cries.

I hated darkness.

I fumbled around until my hand found the wall around the door. I touched all along the sides, worrying when nothing happened until I remembered that the spot to touch for turning on the light in this place was underneath the door. Searching lower, it still took several minutes to find the right place.

Once the light came up, my heartbeat slowed. I took deep breaths and let them out slowly. The purple dragon was here. Here! I couldn't hear anything, either in my mind or with my ears. Where had Vidar and the other dragon gone? I wondered if Vidar would be able to defeat the monster, now that he was grown, not some twelve-year-old dragon. He'd undoubtedly try.

I wondered how long Vidar would be off chasing the creature. What if the two dragons managed to end each other? I'd be stuck in here, sealed in a sarcophagus of stone. I set my hand on the door to be sure, but as expected, nothing moved.

"Wonderful. I guess I'll just stay here, then."

I re-explored the cube. The farm implements hung neatly on their pegs. Seeds sat quietly in their bags and casks. There was nothing out of place and nothing to do. No kitchen, no loom, not even a set of carding combs or knitting needles. I explored every square inch of the place and opened every cask and bag. My spirits lifted when I found a book in a drawer of the planting table next to the seed stacks. The neighbors had always told my father he was foolish to teach his daughters to read and cipher, but he'd said that even women should be able to read the Good

Book, and it wouldn't hurt them to know their numbers, either. I sent up a little prayer of thanks for that as I opened the book, hoping it was something that could occupy my mind, at least for a time. Unfortunately, my excitement was short-lived. The book was merely a ledger and planting calendar, similar to the one my father kept—had kept—in the barn.

Its old-fashioned script detailed lists that corresponded precisely to the items in the barn. Almost too precisely. The number of small stone pots was listed as twenty-two. I ran back to the pile of pots where I'd found the ones I'd filled with dirt yesterday and counted those that remained. Exactly twenty-two. But I'd taken a hundred from this pile. How could the ledger know what I'd taken? Was it magically keeping track? What would happen if I broke something? Not an important tool, of course. I looked around, and my eye caught on a set of small garden stakes. That would work. I counted them. One hundred fifty. I found their spot in the ledger. One hundred fifty. I broke one over my knee. As I did so, the number fogged and then reappeared as one hundred forty-nine.

I breathed in sharply. Amazing. I'd heard of magical books, of course, but now I held one in my hands. A pity its contents weren't more interesting. Still, it was something to look at while I waited for Vidar to return. If Vidar returned. I wouldn't think about that. I focused on the ledger.

After reading the thing cover to cover four times, I had half the contents memorized and couldn't bring myself to start again. I returned the book to its drawer and explored the space again. I found everything the ledger said I would find and nothing else.

I tried the door again. It remained firmly shut. "Vidar, where are you?"

Silence was my only answer.

My stomach growled. I supposed I could eat some of the seed, but I couldn't imagine what my father would have said if he learned I was even thinking of eating seed grain. He'd probably find some way to come back from the dead to lecture me. I wasn't that hungry. Yet.

Perhaps I could sleep. I set some cloth sacks on the floor. They weren't much of a cushion, but they at least blocked a bit of the cold of the stone.

I lay on them, first on my side, then on my back, then the other side, then my front, cushioning my head in my hands. I couldn't get comfortable in any position. The light didn't help.

I dragged the bags next to the entrance, settled myself back on them, and touched the wall to bring the darkness back.

Even in the dark, it took a horribly long time to fall asleep. Perhaps it wasn't really time for rest yet. Or perhaps there was too much on my mind for me to sleep well.

At last, I drifted off, but in my dreams, I wandered a sterile marble maze with no exit. I woke screaming in the dark to find my reality little better than the dream.

Still, I was reluctant to return to sleep. I sat with my back against the door and hugged my knees, trying to think of nothing at all.

I must have drifted off to sleep again, for at some point, I woke with a start and found my skirt dampened at the knee where I'd been drooling. I slapped the wall behind me until the light came up, stretching until the ache of sleeping cramped against stone was worked out. I folded the bags I'd slept on and put them away before locating a large bucket to use as a chamber pot.

Then I cast about for something to keep me occupied. Unfortunately, there wasn't a single tool or supply that needed to be prepared, aside from the stake I'd broken, and that was past fixing. There were seeds that could be planted, but no dirt to plant them in and not enough light to grow them once they were planted.

The drawer with the ledger held two charcoal sticks, but no paper. I supposed I could write on a wall. But write what?

I decided to draw a plan of the farm, mapping out the river, buildings, orchards, vineyard, pastures and fields, the glass-blowing area, and the little paths. I hadn't realized how big the place was until I had the map of it stretched across an entire wall of the barn. Four or five times the size of my family farm, it was enormous. How could one family work all this?

Of course, I'd seen Vidar working. He'd put up the greenhouse in less than a week. Perhaps this was no more than several dragons could handle.

I wished the orchards were more than blackened stumps. They must have been so pretty when the blooms were out in the spring. If Vidar ever came back, I'd tell him that was what we should work on next—the orchards. If they went in now, I might yet live to see them in their full glory. If the purple dragon didn't keep destroying them, that was.

I dropped the charcoal back in the drawer with the ledger and rubbed my hands to try to remove the dark smudges there. I could sure use one of those magic spigots now. There wasn't a drop of water in this place—nothing to clean with, and nothing to drink.

Suddenly, I was very thirsty. My mouth felt both dry and swollen. My throat was parched. How had I not noticed this before?

To distract myself, I pulled out the ledger and forced myself to reread it. The pages smudged where I turned them, so I was careful to avoid touching any words or numbers. I read. And read. When my mind flitted off three times in the same line, I started reading aloud. That kept me focused on the task a little better, even if I felt silly declaiming a list of farm supplies.

I wondered how long I had been locked in here. Hours? Days? Where was Vidar?

The ledger slipped from my fingers, and I realized I'd stopped reading. I picked the book up and restarted from the last point I could remember clearly.

When I came to the end of the ledger, I tried reciting passages from the Good Book. When I couldn't remember any more, I sang all the songs I knew.

By then, I was so exhausted, I tried sleeping again, but every time I slipped into sleep, the marble maze dream plagued me. Each time I woke from it, I felt more panicked than the time before.

Finally, I sat again, back against the wall, knees drawn up. My stomach flapped hollowly. My mouth yearned for liquid.

Something must have happened to Vidar. Otherwise, he would come to me. I just hoped he managed to take out the purple dragon in this fight. If that monster had died, it didn't matter what happened to me. I could die here, happy, if only I knew the purple beast was also gone. I pictured it, imagining the two giants of armor and fire battling over the hills. Purple and black wrestled, wreathed in multicolored fire and smoke thick as clouds. I imagined Vidar's claw piercing straight through the purple monster's throat and the beasts plunging downward together, crashing into a mountainside. Tears slipped down my cheeks. I hadn't realized I cared about Vidar that much. It was just a fancy anyway. Who knew what had actually happened to him?

I brushed away my tears and then sucked the salty liquid off my dirty fingers. Part of me was disgusted with myself. The rest of me only knew I was thirsty. Horribly thirsty.

I'm so sorry, Rilla. I would have been back sooner, but that monster ripped my wings.

The door swung open, and light poured in.

CHAPTER TWELVE

Breeze and Stars

he pump was nearer than the river, and I drank from it directly, great gasping gulps that my mother would have chided even my brothers for taking.

Be careful. Drinking too much at one time could cause you to throw up.

At the moment, I didn't care. Well, maybe, I did. I slowed down with the water. When my thirst was finally quenched, and I'd used the outhouse, I finally noticed something besides my own needs. Vidar looked terrible. Half the scales on his right side were cracked. His right wing dragged on the ground as if it was broken, and the membrane in it was as holey as ragged lace.

"Vidar! How can I help?"

I'll heal. I only need a few good meals and a week or two to recover.

"But if you can't fly, how will you hunt?"

I've become very good at stalking prey on foot. It takes time to make a meal of rabbits and mice, but I can do it.

"What if that monster comes back here while you're recovering?"

He did this to me himself, so his wings and scales look every bit as bad as mine. I did some damage of my own as well.

"Enough to kill him?"

Probably not, but he shifted, so he could cast a protective shield, and that will slow his healing. I don't think we'll need to worry about him for a month or two. We have time. Eat something and get changed. I'll find something for myself. It will be easier to face the mess on full stomachs.

"The mess?" Now, I remembered the crashes I'd heard before Vidar's voice disappeared. "What did he destroy? Are the sheep all right?"

As if in answer to my call, Tyrant, Buster, Little Lady, Blackie, Fern, and Dancer came running around the corner of the building and greeted us with almost painful enthusiasm. I was jostled back and forth such that I could hardly keep my footing. I didn't care. If the sheep were all right, we could fix the rest. I petted Fern. "How did they escape?"

They were off by the river when Adramelech attacked. I'm not sure he even saw them.

"Adramelech is the name of the purple dragon?"

Yes. Vidar spat over the sheep's heads onto the ground, where his sputum sizzled and then burnt out.

"But Adramelech did destroy things."

Eat first. It's easier to handle things on a full stomach.

I had no idea if that was true or not, and I had some worry that a full stomach might just make for more to come back up when I eventually saw the destruction, but I heeded his advice. It was easier than arguing.

While I ate, washed up, and changed clothes, Vidar slipped away. Even without the full use of his wings, he moved lightning fast, and I wasn't at all surprised when he returned shortly after I'd finished my bath. He carried a young buck and a brace of rabbits that looked like their necks had been snapped. He made remarkably short work of all three animals. It wasn't quite as fast as when Adramelech swallowed a person or cow whole, but nearly.

Once he'd eaten, Vidar took a long drink from the river and then let out a puff of steam that fogged half the basin. *I suppose we'd best be getting on with it.*

I followed Vidar to a knoll that overlooked the greenhouse we'd made, but instead of the greenhouse, the spot was once again a heap of broken rock and shattered glass.

As I stared at it, my heart unaccountably lightened. "That's it?"

What do you mean? Isn't it enough?

"But we know how to fix that," I said. "It will be right as rain again in a week—well, maybe, a bit more since you can't use your wings. It's not like he got any people or animals or trees—nothing living or ancient or irreplaceable."

I hadn't thought of it that way, but you are right.

"Of course, I am. And aren't you glad we put all the tools away each night? I'll go get the wheelbarrow."

The next few days were long and full of hard work, but my muscles ached less than they had the first time we'd cleaned up the stones. Vidar, too, seemed to be moving faster, even though his wings still had more holes than membrane. The holes were smaller than they had been, and the right wing had straightened. It appeared strong when Vidar flung it out for balance when he leapt from rubble pile to staging area with a giant rock clutched in his claws.

I slept well at nights except when the marble maze dream visited me. The first time that woke me, I left the bunk and went out to look at the stars.

Do you want to talk about it?

I really didn't.

How long have you been having that nightmare?

"Since I was trapped in the barn."

Vidar looked troubled. *I should have returned more quickly.*

"Could you have returned more quickly?"

Maybe if I hadn't chased Adramelech as long. But until he fell out of the sky and changed, I expected him to double back and attack again.

"He probably would have. You needed to go that far. And being in the barn saved my life. I just wish there had been food and water and a better bed."

And a toilet? I am not sure how to make those, but my father will have left instructions.

"In the library in Dragonhome," I said. "Which we can't get to right now because you can't fly. We'll worry about it another time." I looked up at the stars. It wasn't the lack of outhouse or food and water that bothered me, I knew. I'd felt the same in Dragonhome, where there was plenty of everything I might need. What bothered me was the feeling of being trapped.

But the barn isn't fireproof when the door is open. And neither is Dragonhome.

"A quick burn might be a better way to go than being buried alive."

You were never buried!

"A larger, more richly appointed coffin than most, perhaps, but still a coffin."

Vidar snorted.

We would never agree on this. He obviously felt at home inside mountains. I never would.

Never?

"I might be all right if I could leave whenever I wanted."

We will search out how to ensure that before we look for instructions on building washrooms.

I smiled. "Fair enough." I leaned against Vidar's side and felt the heat of him, even through his sides. The stars twinkled overhead, and I breathed deeply, expanding my lungs. What a pity Dragonhome couldn't be out here near the stars and the breeze.

I never cared much about stars and breeze, but I'm beginning to see their attraction.

The next day, we finished clearing the rubble, and Vidar's wings were healed enough that he thought he might be able to make glass again.

This time, while he blew the glass, I looked for stones the right size for pots to replace the ones that had been smashed. Clay ones could have worked as well, but I'd never been much of a potter, and Vidar said the markets were too far for us to go with him in his current state, but that he could shape stones for us to use.

Before he could shape any stones, either for the greenhouse or my pots, he needed another meal. Since I'd already found all the stones we'd need the first day he worked on glass, I promised to find something for him while he kept working.

You? How will you catch anything to eat?

"I thought I'd take the snares and that bow and arrow set from the bunkhouse and try my luck in the forest." I pointed toward the western slope of our basin.

Who taught you to hunt?

"No one taught me, exactly. When I was younger, I used to follow my older brothers everywhere and copy them. I soon learned to be silent and invisible, so they couldn't catch me and send me home. And it turned out that helped with the hunting. How they used to hate it when I came home with more game than they did."

I would imagine. Well, it wouldn't hurt for you to try. Just stay within hailing distance.

I promised I would and set out to explore the mountains on the far side of the basin. The walk there took nearly an hour, and it felt good to move with a quick stride, not bent over, looking for rocks. The sheep followed me at first, but when I passed the last of the meadows and moved into a grove of pine trees, they stayed behind, bleating pitifully.

"I'll return as soon as I can," I told them. "Vidar needs food."

This seemed to satisfy them, for they scattered through the meadow and picked at the grass.

Setting snares was easy, but it took a while for me to find any larger game, and even longer to hunt it down, for my first arrow went wide of its mark and spooked the small group of elk I was tailing. I tracked them for two more hours before I got myself close enough to try again.

This time my aim was true, and I brought down the largest of the small herd. I didn't realize how large it was until I approached and realized I'd never be able to carry it back to the farm.

"Vidar?" I said softly.

Yes, my love.

"Your what?"

I mean, yes, Rilla?

"You called me your love."

Weren't you going to ask me if I could come get that elk you've brought down?

"I was, but—"

I'll be there as soon as I can.

"Vidar? Vidar?"

The frustrating beast wouldn't answer. What on earth did he mean by calling me his love? I sat down next to the elk. Annoying dragon. I wondered how long I'd have to wait. It would take me close to three hours to reach this point from the farm, going directly, but Vidar moved faster than I did.

Much faster. He was there surprisingly fast—perhaps ten minutes. In another ten minutes, he'd polished off the animal.

When he'd finished, he curled up next to me. *Thank you. That was very good.*

"You're welcome. I'm sorry I couldn't bring it back to you."

Do not worry about it. You gave me time to finish the glass.

"Finish? It took three days last time."

I'm much faster now.

Clearly. I sat next to him, leaning up against his side. "Why did you call me your love?"

Because I love you.

He loved me? We still barely knew each other.

We have been living together for a few weeks now. That is plenty of time for a dragon to form a bond.

~ 74 ~

A bond? Vidar had formed a bond with me? Would it tie me to him even more securely than the slave-brand he'd marked me with?

A bond doesn't tie you to me, it ties me to you.

I failed to see the difference.

It's probably safer for me that way.

"Safer for you? You're a dragon. How could I hurt you?"

The same way any woman can hurt a man who loves her, little one.

I thought about how miserable Khan had been when the girl he liked in the village had told him she was going to marry some rich man from the city. Yes, I suppose Vidar might be sad if I went off with someone else, but I wasn't sure that was the same thing as danger. Besides, I wasn't planning on going anywhere. I wasn't even sure I could. I had no idea how far it was to the next town, nor in which direction it lay.

Westmarket is forty miles that way. Vidar pointed. *But if you desire to go there, I can fly you. You might not survive a trip on foot through the mountain passes this time of year.*

"You would take me just because I wished to go?"

I love you. I will not keep you here if you wish to go.

I breathed in a deep gulp of the pine-scented air. "But when I first came, you said I had to stay. That I was your sacrifice."

That was wrong of me. It was so good to talk to someone else after so many years that I forgot everything my parents taught me about relationships.

"How long has it been, Vidar?"

Two hundred seventy-four years.

I sucked in a deep breath. Two hundred seventy-four?

Ah, well. It wasn't like I had any relatives or even friends to go home to. I might as well stay and keep Vidar company.

You are very generous.

"Hardly."

I think I have rested enough. I will head back now. Would you like me to carry you?

"No, thank you." I preferred walking when that was possible. Besides, I wanted to check my snares.

Fair enough.

Vidar took off with a flying leap, but his wings still looked ragged. I hoped he wouldn't push himself too hard.

For you, I will be careful.

Silly dragon.

I smiled as I started back the way I'd come, keeping away from the slick patches of unmelted snow behind boulders and under trees.

I found three rabbits and a raccoon in my snares. Not bad for a day of hunting, I thought as I collected the empty snares along with the full ones. The traps looked like the ones my brothers and I made, but I'd found them on the walls of the sleeping hut, and I wondered if some dragon magic lingered on them. Surely, I'd never been so successful in such a short time with a line of snares before.

The sun was setting by the time I returned to the farm, footsore but relaxed. Vidar was happy to take two of the rabbits and the coon, but he insisted I clean the last rabbit for myself and started up a fire for me to roast it.

Rabbit roasted in dragon flame had a tangy, smoked flavor. I wasn't sure I'd ever had a meal so good as that rabbit with wild carrots and stream water. I sat, leaning against Vidar's side, late into the night, watching the fire die down and the stars come out.

My mother liked rabbit, too. Vidar's thoughts drifted toward me after we'd sat in quiet companionship for what felt like hours. *And stars as well.*

"A woman with fine taste, then. And clever with her needles if those sweaters were her work."

Oh, yes. She always made us sweaters. Vidar chuckled. *She used to get so angry when we ruined them.*

"Why did you?"

We boys couldn't always control when we turned into dragons. And no sweater could stand up to the change. If they didn't shred with the growth, they would char.

I remembered the half-finished sweater in the basket by the hearth in Dragonhome. It was just the right size for a twelve-year-old. I gasped. "Your other form is human!"

The golden chains in my mind descended so quickly, I barely had time to see them before blackness overtook me.

CHAPTER THIRTEEN

Orchard

When I returned to awareness, bright sun shone down on me, and I could hear Vidar over by the greenhouse, moving boulders. My head ached, but I could still remember the conversation from the night before. Vidar was…

My headache increased tenfold. Perhaps it would be best not to pursue that line of thinking—at least for the moment.

I ate a bit of leftover rabbit, bathed in the stream, and petted the sheep. Then I sought out Vidar.

The first level of wall in the greenhouse was already up, and the collar around Vidar's neck had as much black as gold. Would it split off completely soon? What would happen when it did? Would Vidar still be the same person when the collar did not restrain him? Surely, he would. Nothing Adramelech had created would affect one in the important ways—handling one's passions and anger responsibly.

You are remarkably wise, my Rilla.

I didn't know about that. But I did know Vidar had made incredible progress while I lay unconscious.

I've become faster at this, too.

"Too fast for help?"

Help is always welcome.

As I gathered a wheelbarrow of filler stones, I asked Vidar if we could handle the orchards next.

The orchards are important, but I think my wings are now strong enough for the return trip to Dragonhome. We should go back and learn what we can about doors, so you can go through them. I will feel better if the safe places for you to hide are also places you can escape from if that becomes necessary.

He was right, of course. "But I thought Adramelech would need a month or more to recover. Couldn't we at least plant a few trees before returning?" Even with the prospect of finding a way to escape, I was in no hurry to bury myself back in the heart of the mountain.

I forget that what feels safe to me feels dangerous to you. I do not wish to rush you. Perhaps there is time enough to plant a few trees before we go.

The greenhouse was back in fine form by the end of the day, and the next day, Vidar turned stones into little pots while I filled them with compost and planted a new set of vegetables and herbs.

"How will they stay moist while we are gone, though?"

That spell, my father taught me. Vidar scratched at his collar, as if it was pulling too tight. *I believe I have enough magic at my disposal to pull it off.*

Vidar placed a claw on the top of the greenhouse roof and poked his snout through the door. Then he closed his eyes and blew a puff of green steam into the greenhouse. He blew and blew until the whole structure was full of the green cloud.

Then he pulled his snout back out and quickly shut the door. Inside the greenhouse, the green steam slowly paled and thickened near the top. The mist lower down thinned and cleared, so the greenhouse looked as though it had a blanket of white clouds floating up near its roof. As I watched, the clouds darkened to gray and then black. Then, with a crack like the voice of a large drum, the clouds rained themselves out into nothing.

There. It is finished. The rains will come once a day now.

"Amazing."

It's impressive, isn't it? My father told me that the best dragons could do this with a whole continent.

"A continent?"

The land between seas.

"You can control the weather?"

Well, I've never tried anywhere beyond this basin.

"You control the weather here?"

Well, yes. Vidar's scales rippled.

"And you're embarrassed by this?"

If I were doing my job, this place wouldn't still be a ruin.

I looked around at the rubble and fallow fields. The grass grew thick and long, and I could tell it would be beautifully green come spring. "But you didn't need the farm. And you're also protecting our border with Arkon, are you not? Didn't you tell me that—something about patching the hole Adramelech made when he burst through and keeping the wall in good repair? And you've been doing it with limited magic?"

Well, yes. I have been doing that.

"Then there's nothing to be embarrassed about. You had to choose, and you chose what would be most important, not just for you, but also for others. And it looks like you've done enough here to keep it fertile. It's going to be a wonderful farm."

I've forgotten how to farm.

"I haven't. Besides, I'm sure your father left instructions."

Vidar chuckled. *I'm sure he did. Well, we'd best get your trees planted, so we can find what he left us.*

I'd seen my father and brothers deal with tree stumps, and each one was a major job, requiring hours of work and at least one ox. Vidar, though, pulled the stumps out of the ground as if they were weeds in a vegetable garden. I wasn't sure if the job was so easy because he was a dragon or because the stumps had been there so long their roots had rotted. Whatever the reason, in less time than I could have imagined, the orchard had been cleared. Vidar stacked the old wood on the compost pile and blew a green steam over the heap. The old wood crumbled, leaving a dark loam in its place.

"Will that be as good for the new trees as I think it will?"

Vidar shrugged, a movement that rolled from his shoulders down the whole length of his body in a sinuous wave.

I watched the wave make its way all the way to the end of his tail before addressing him again. "We'll need a hole for each tree. We'll refill the holes with earth mixed with this compost. It'll mound up a little, and I suspect that will be perfect for the saplings."

Tell me where to put the holes and how big to make them.

"About as big as the wheelbarrow," I said. "I'll set a stone marker where I want the center of each tree."

I set the stones about where the old trees had been. Someone had spaced them remarkably well. They seemed a bit far apart at the moment, but full-grown trees needed space.

Vidar followed along behind me, scooping out one or two claw-fulls of dirt in each spot. By nightfall, we'd placed all the holes.

The next day, we mixed dirt, filled the holes, and planted seeds—apple, cherry, pear, peach, crabapple, and apricot. When we finished, the evenly spaced, bare mounds of earth looked hopeful.

Yes, but there are no grapes.

"Oh, right. You like raisins. I marked a vineyard on my map, but I was just guessing on the placement. Where was the original?"

Vidar led me over to a large field full of fist-sized rubble.

"Let me guess. Your arbors were stone?"

It's best to make as much as possible from stone when there are young dragons about.

I moved closer to the old vineyard. "This was hit hard."

Adramelech found it easier to break than some things. And my father loved raisins almost as much as I do.

Vindictive beast. The horrible creature didn't seem to know how to do anything except destroy what others had made.

It is easier to destroy than create, and both destruction and creation are easier than restoring what has been broken.

I reached down and picked up a rock from the vineyard rubble. Its curve suggested it had once been part of an arch. "Do we have time to restore this before going down to Dragonhome?"

I would rather not put it together just so Adramelech can take it apart again. When I have learned better how to protect it, I'll be ready to work on it. I will see if I can spell the weather for this basin, though. It has shifted some since my father was able to attend to it. Vidar sucked in a deep breath and then let out a cloud of green steam that thickened and swirled around us. It was warm and wet, but not caustic, the way I expected green steam to be.

Vidar kept blowing and blowing, for what felt like hours until without warning, he stopped. *Now, we wait.*

At first, nothing happened. Then, just as in the greenhouse, the green fog rose upward, thickening and growing paler as it moved upward until a thick blanket of white clouds sat above us, cutting off the mountains two-thirds of the way up their sides. The clouds darkened. I was so fascinated with the process that I forgot what came next until a gentle rain soaked my hair and clothes. I laughed. "I guess I needed to clean up."

I, too, needed the shower. Well, I'm glad this is working. I had best sleep. I'll hunt in the morning before we return to Dragonhome. Vidar scratched at his collar. Several of the black cracks in it looked as if they were halfway through, but the itching still didn't appear to have any effect, at least not on the collar. The scales around it looked worn and dull.

"Stop scratching. It's wearing down your scales."

I can't help it. Whenever I do magic, this infernal thing itches like crazy.

"But you're wearing down your scales there. Can you afford to have weak protection on your neck?"

Vidar dropped his claw. *I didn't realize.*

"You can't feel the difference?"

I can only feel the collar there.

"Part of the magic, I suppose. If it's annoying enough, you'd be significantly weakened by the time you managed to get the thing off. Unless the scales can grow stronger."

Not quickly. I will refrain from scraping them, however provoked I am. Thank you.

He stared at me, and I felt immersed in the emerald gaze again. He had such beautiful eyes. I reached a hand up to cup his cheek and was surprised when I touched the hard scales of his snout. Somehow, I'd expected to feel human skin, to lean into the embrace of a human man.

Gold glinted in my mind, and I fought it back. I would not let those chains fall. Not today. Not when I felt so close to discovering something important, something crucial. A headache split the space between my ears, but I ignored that, too.

Water dripped into my eyes, and the moment passed. I dropped my hand, hardly remembering why I'd lifted it in the first place. "I should get into dry clothes."

Yes, Vidar thought. Even though the word existed only in my mind, it sounded breathless, unlike the rest of Vidar's words. Odd. Very, very odd.

I turned to look at him twice on the way back to the bunkhouse.

Both times, he stood stock-still, gazing at me, his eyes glowing with a message I could see as clearly as I could hear the thoughts he sent my way.

His eyes said, "I love you."

CHAPTER FOURTEEN

 woke late, having slept fitfully, and found, to my dismay, that Vidar had already finished his hunting and was waiting to carry me back to Dragonhome. I hurried through my breakfast, said goodbye to the sheep, changed back into the clothes I'd worn the first day on the farm, and washed the work clothes, hanging them in the bunkhouse to be ready for the next time we came this way. Surely, there would be a next time.

Of course, my Rilla. You seem to need your sunshine and fresh air as much as I need the darkness and feel of earth above my head.

He liked the darkness and feeling of being underground?

I am a dragon.

I hadn't realized dragons liked the underground so much. I felt selfish for keeping him in the open air for so long.

Above ground is all right, too. I don't dislike the farm the way you dislike Dragonhome. You seem to shrink from being beneath the ground.

"But you feel exposed."

We ARE exposed aboveground. But it must happen some if I am to hunt—or farm. With you to look after, I find the farming as important as the hunting. And someday, I will break this collar, and

I, too, will eat fruits and grains again. Still, I will be glad to return to the earth and rest a bit.

Vidar needed rest. He seemed thinner than when I'd first met him, and his wings were still a bit ragged. If he could appreciate being out in the open for my sake, I could try to appreciate Dragonhome for his.

Maybe being underground was unpleasant, but the magical water spigots were wonderful. I couldn't wait to take another warm bath. And make a fresh batch of bread. Magically preserved bread was all well and fine, but there was nothing quite like the smell of bread in the oven.

Very true. I am looking forward to that even if I no longer eat bread. Smelling it is nearly as good. Before I brought you home, I hadn't smelled bread in so long, I'd forgotten what it was like. When I am a man again, I'm not sure what I will eat first—raisins or bread.

At the word "man," a spurt of pain and a glimmer of gold shot through my mind, but I ignored them both, focusing hard on staying aware and upright. Man. Vidar's other form was human. Which made sense, given that his mother was human. It felt so obvious. Of course, he was a man when he wasn't a dragon. Why would Sir Drake want to keep me from that information?

My headache increased in size and intensity, and the golden chains started to fall.

"No," I shouted. "I am mistress of my own mind!"

❧ ☙

Apparently, I wasn't, for I came to myself in the pearly cave outside Dragonhome, Vidar's long snout inches from my face. *Oh, good. You're up. And you seem to have all your faculties.*

I struggled to sit up, and Vidar backed away to give me room. "I hate this."

I do, too.

"How long was I…unaware?"

A few hours this time. I think you are breaking Sir Drake's mind chains as surely as I am breaking his collar. But there's no need to push it. Perhaps you should rest for a bit. Get that bath you wanted.

"You'll keep the door open?"

Whenever I am in the outer chamber.

That was good. I crept through the entrance tunnel and turned on the lights. Dragonhome welcomed me with homey warmth.

My bath was long and luxurious, and I dried my hair in front of a roaring fire before sinking into the unbelievable softness of the giant, green-clothed bed.

The next day, I took my time with another bath and a batch of bread, but after a few hours, I sought out Vidar to see what he wanted me to look for in the library.

He was flying out in the giant cave part of Dragonhome, swooping through and around majestic columns, now sideways, now upright, now upside down. I sat and watched in awe and building joy. So beautiful.

Vidar glided to a stop before me. *Do you really think so?*

"I thought you could tell what I was thinking."

Vidar bared his teeth, and I wasn't sure whether he meant to smile or snarl.

Smile. That was definitely a smile.

"If you say so."

He shook his head. *Did you need something?*

"I was wondering what I should look for in the library. Dragon marks, doors, farming, magical water pumps, and outhouses—"

And protection. I suspect we'll need more of that.

I nodded. "Would you like me to bring the books out here, so you can look at them?"

He tipped his head to one side. *I suppose that is best, but it's difficult to read with these eyes.*

"I could read them to you."

You can read?

"Papa thought it was important for all his children to be able to read."

Ah. So did my father. Well, in that case, perhaps it's best if you read them to me.

I could do that. I headed back into the library to see if I could find what we needed.

There's a leather-bound ledger in the desk that should help you.

I found the ledger easily, and soon got lost in perusing the titles and short descriptions. There were more books here than I had ever seen. I stroked the leather covers and sniffed the old pages, getting a breath full of dust that started a sneezing fit.

Rilla! Are you all right?

"Fine. Nothing hurt but my pride."

Why would your pride—never mind. You probably don't want to answer that.

He was a remarkably sensitive dragon—not that I had lots of examples to compare him to.

Anyone would look good next to Adramelech. He's one of the worst of our kind.

"ONE of the worst?" I squeaked.

Probably the worst living dragon aside from Renove, king of Arkon.

Renove was a name I'd heard whispered in nightmare tales around campfires. I'd always imagined he was a myth, a legend conjured to scare small children into good behavior.

A very real legend, I'm afraid, but not one we need to worry about. He's too lazy to step much beyond his castle in Arkon, and my father chose this place, in part, because it is beyond Renove's reach.

"What if Renove's reach has grown?"

I would feel a change in his power pulsing on the wall my father built between Dragonhome and Arkon.

That reassured me, at least some. Adramelech was enough of a threat to worry about. Not that worrying ever accomplished anything, as my mother used to say. I returned to the task at hand—finding books.

The ledger helped me find a whole section of books on agriculture, sitting next to shelves and shelves about weather.

My family has always been weather dragons. Weather and watcher dragons, actually.

That explained the greenhouse magic. I looked at the agricultural shelves in front of me. It would take years to read through all these.

We have time. Perhaps we should start with a good overview—or a couple of them.

I nodded and located an animal husbandry primer, a book on fields and forests, one on maintaining soil, one on orchards, and a final one on vineyards.

You don't want to look up tending vegetable gardens?

"I already know enough about that to be getting on with."

Books on running water were harder to find. I finally ran down some instructions in an old journal with no title that appeared to be Vidar's father's notes on how he'd built Dragonhome. The writing was spidery and old-fashioned, but with work, I could make it out. Vidar was so excited about the connection to his father that I read the journal first, sitting in the entrance tunnel to the human part of Dragonhome with the light from within spilling over my shoulders.

We read the book cover to cover, and in addition to the magic for running water and preserving food, I learned how much Vidar's father had loved his mother and how dangerous it was each time she bore a new dragon. I learned about Vidar's brothers and sisters and how proud their parents were of them all, even Vidar, who they regarded as an absolute baby.

Long before we finished and I closed the book, Vidar had curled up in a ball, tears flowing down his snout to collect in a pool on the cavern floor.

"Do you want me to stop?"

No. It is good to remember them.

I had never seen any man cry that way—not that Vidar was a man, exactly. Well, he would be sometime if the collar didn't keep him always a dragon. Maybe dragon men were more emotional than the more normal men I was familiar with.

We aren't. But neither do we have to prove we're big and tough. Anybody can see that, just by looking at us. Even in our human forms.

I smiled and went back to reading. When I'd finished the book, I was more than ready for dinner and another rest.

The next day, we started our research earlier since I still had plenty of bread left from my last batch and didn't need to make more. No matter how I looked, though, I couldn't find anything that collected information on dragon marks.

We'll need to pull it out of the spell books, then.

"The spell books?"

They'll be locked in the cabinet behind the desk.

I was sitting at the desk, looking at the ledger, so I turned around. "What cabinet?" All I could see was a smooth stone wall.

You don't even see the lock?

I shook my head, not that Vidar could see me.

It should be there. A black dragon on an emerald seal.

"No. Nothing but a white wall."

Vidar growled so loudly that I heard him with my ears, not my mind, even though I was down in the quiet library. I ducked down under the desk and covered my head.

Rilla? Rilla? I'm so sorry. I didn't mean to frighten you. It's all right. That was just noise.

"Noise that sounded like it could bring down the mountain."

No—of course not. Well, at least I don't think so. My father used to say that the biggest dragons could bring down a mountain just by growling, but I'm hardly one of the biggest.

"You're as big around as Adramelech, and a good bit longer."

I suppose I might be. But how would you know? You haven't seen us together.

"I know how to judge distances," I said as I crawled out from under the desk. "Adramelech was the length of our upper pasture. You're longer. At any rate, what now?"

If we can't get at the spell books, we may be able to find what we need in the histories. Some of the stories explain how things are done.

"Histories?" I looked at the wall dedicated to them. If we had to dig through all that, I doubted we'd find a solution to the door problem in my lifetime.

We know a solution, Vidar thought crossly. *You just don't like it.*

"We do? What solution?"

You could become my wife. The wife mark opens all doors.

Oh. He had said that before. Or at least implied it. But he was a dragon. One who couldn't change form. "Maybe we should try some of the histories."

Yes. Vidar's voice sounded weary.

"I do like you, Vidar. I'm just not sure I'm ready to…"

I understand. I do not want to push you.

No, he was much too sweet to push anyone. I pulled one of the giant histories off the shelf. "How do we know which one to start with?"

Vidar listed a few titles, including the one I'd just grabbed, and I retrieved them, bringing the lot out to the main room to join the pile of agricultural books I'd found.

Reading the histories was more fun than reading about trees or tending sheep, but it brought us no closer to a solution to the door problem that didn't involve me becoming Vidar's wife.

After about a week of looking, Vidar needed to hunt, and I wanted to check on the sheep and the greenhouse, so we headed back up to the farm. We would be busy since we also planned to plow the land for grain, but we carried a few of the books up with us to read in the evenings.

Plowing had always looked like hard work, but with Vidar pulling the plow, it was less exhausting than I expected. My arms ached from the vibration of the handle by the end of the day, but the hardest thing was keeping up with Vidar's pace—and getting the mud out of my skirts. I suspected Vidar didn't really need my help—unless it was for an extra pair of eyes behind him to keep the rows straight. And to drop the seeds in, of course. Vidar's claws couldn't handle that delicate task.

After the sun set, we read together by the light of the fire, and I learned of dragon kings, dragon loves, dragon laws, dragon traitors, and dragon wars. I also learned of dragon slaves—humans set to work in dragon households and frequently used to feed all kinds of dragon appetites.

My dragon mark was most assuredly a slave mark.

Vidar's scales fluttered in embarrassment the first time I became sure of this—and every time we read about slaves thereafter.

I didn't know, his thoughts whispered into my mind when we were reading one of the uglier of these passages.

"How could you not know?"

You heard that? I didn't mean for you to hear that.

"I heard. And you haven't answered my question."

When my father taught me this mark, he called it something else.

"Not a slave mark?"

No. He said it was abominable to make slaves.

"What did he say you were making?"

Pets. He said this mark created Dragonpets.

"Pets?! You think I'm a pet?" My shriek was shrill enough that Vidar covered his ears.

"I can't talk to you right now." I set the book next to me on the stone I'd been using as a seat and struggled to my feet. I needed to be away from the fire, away from the farm, away from Vidar. He didn't follow me as I slipped past the fields and under the trees. Nor did he think into my mind.

Still, I could feel his dejection. It settled over the valley, thicker than a fog.

CHAPTER FIFTEEN

Sickness

verhead, lightning flashed, and thunder rumbled. The evening rains misted downward, dripping through the trees and plopping down like giant tears, and I had to remind myself that this was the normal evening fall of water for the farm, not some petulant dragon fit.

At least, I didn't think it was. No voice interrupted my thoughts to confirm or correct my assumptions. I wandered through the crying trees, so soaked through with Vidar's sorrow that it might have been my own.

And why wouldn't it be my sorrow as well? What did I have in the world anymore besides Vidar and Dragonhome, and the farm here? I stopped, sank to my knees, and cried as I'd never cried before.

Dark fell before I'd finished my cry. I lifted myself from my knees, brushed off my hands, and looked for a more comfortable spot to sit and think—not that anyplace would be comfortable in my sodden clothing as the air rapidly cooled.

I stumbled through the clearing until I found a couple of boulders that were no damper than my clothes. I scrambled atop one, tucked my knees to my chest, and shivered as I tried to make sense of my feelings.

Anger—it still bubbled hot beneath my sorrow, but not so violently as when I'd confronted Vidar on the farm.

How could he have thought that having a pet was better or even different than making a person a slave?

We're obligated to love pets.

"And you don't need to love slaves?"

Keeping slaves is evil.

"I agree with you, but I don't see how changing the name makes it less evil."

It's not the same thing.

"No?"

Pets don't have to work for you.

"All my father's dogs worked—hunting or herding sheep. The cats controlled the rodent population."

I imagined something more like one of the palace pets.

"You thought I'd be like one of the palace girl's yippy little lap dogs? Weak, whiny, and useless?"

Of course not.

"Oh, then like one of those birds in a gilded cage—beautiful, but sadly mutilated?"

No! I thought—I don't know what I thought. I needed to get you inside, and I was afraid to give you a wife mark.

"Afraid? Because you thought I might hurt you?"

If I bonded to you, and you never bonded to me, it would slowly destroy me. It is slowly destroying me.

"What are you talking about? You didn't give me a wife mark."

No. But I appear to have bonded to you all the same. A mark isn't required for it to happen. I remember my father telling me about it once, shortly before the end. I didn't pay much attention. It all seemed silly then—that a woman could become so much more important than anything else, even Dragonhome.

I thought of him as a boy listening to his father talk about women and love. When Khan was twelve summers, he'd sworn he would never have anything to do with women when he grew up. I smiled. "You were young. Naturally, you didn't understand."

It has been a long time since I was young. I should know better now.

I sneezed.

You are wet and cold. Please come back to the farm to get warm and dry. If you still want to leave tomorrow, I will take you to the nearest town.

"What will happen to you if I go?"

I will miss you, of course. But it would be far worse to keep you here against your will. I do not like to think about what I would become if I did that.

I was glad he felt that way. I sneezed again and thought Vidar was right about the value of getting warm and dry. I could decide what I felt about all this and what I wanted to do in the morning. I struggled up from the rock I'd found, looked about me, and realized I had no idea where I was, nor could I see well enough to guess which way was toward the farm and which was away.

Don't worry. I'll find you.

I shrank in on myself, shivering and sneezing, but sooner than I hoped for, Vidar slipped into the clearing, his scales glowing like they had when he first took me down to Dragonhome. He offered to carry me back to the farm, and I probably should have let him, but I couldn't, somehow, in that moment, entrust myself to his claws. It was some time since Vidar had seemed monstrous to me, but there in the dark, as I stumbled along behind the twinkle of green, I couldn't help shuddering from time to time. Maybe it was merely the cold. Part of me insisted that despite this most recent disagreement, Vidar was nothing like Adramelech. Much of the rest of me just wanted warm clothes and my comfortable bunk.

In due time, we made it back to the farm, and the wished-for clothes and bunk were every bit as comfortable as I'd imagined. Sleep claimed me almost the moment I lay down.

When morning came, I felt feverish, and my sniffles had grown into a feeling that my head was stuffed with wool. I couldn't remember the last time I'd stayed abed when there was work to be done, but that morning I did it, giving myself over to fever dreams of dread and sound that I could not escape.

Several times I remember waking, each time to a greater headache. My breathing labored, and I could not find a comfortable position in which to sleep, but neither could I easily force my limbs from the bed. At Vidar's insistence, I drank water and juices from the supplies in the bunkhouse. I could feel panic welling in him, but I couldn't think well enough to make sense of my own feelings, let alone his.

I don't know how long I spent in the haze of sickness, but I do know that there came a day when I couldn't even get up to relieve myself or drink, and I felt Vidar's anguish reverberating throughout the whole valley, stronger even than the fever dreams.

Please, Rilla, let me give you a wife mark. You needn't stay with me if you don't want to, but at least I will know that you are alive somewhere.

The words hardly made sense to me, but I assented. If I didn't need to stay with him, what difference would a wife mark make to me?

As soon as I agreed, I felt my body lift from the bed and float toward the door of the bunkhouse. It must have been magic—powerful magic. I was too exhausted to be impressed or to wonder how Vidar managed such a feat with his collar. I floated out the door, strangely comfortable, though nothing supported me but magic.

Once I was in front of Vidar, he lowered me gently to the ground and touched the point on my collarbone that had the sun marking. Once again, I felt an almost unbearable heat. Warmth suffused my body, starting at that point and spreading outward until it felt as though every part of me, from my hair to my toes, was bursting with light. When I held my hand before my face, it actually glowed. The light became brighter and brighter, almost painfully so, until, in a blaze of glory, it erupted outward from me, shooting visible sparks in every direction.

When the sparks were gone, I ran my hands over my face and my arms, shocked to find all of myself intact, though beneath my skin, I could see faint, twining, green patterns. The unbearable brightness and the warmth had left, and with them had gone my fever and headache. I felt no need to cough or sneeze or even sniffle.

I took in my first deep, unobstructed breath in a long time, and my eyes widened. "You...It..."

The wife mark can heal.

I lifted myself to my feet, surprised to find myself full of energy.

I know you don't want this, but I couldn't think what else to do. I don't know any other way to heal a human.

"I don't know what I want, Vidar," I said. "I haven't had time to think about it since I learned that you'd made me your pet." But I wasn't his pet any longer, was I? I ran to the barn, locked myself inside, and then pressed my hand against the door panel. It swung open.

There is nothing of mine that you cannot open, now.

"Even the bookcase with magic in the library?"

Even that.

A wave of excitement passed over me. Then I remembered that we'd wanted that library so that we could find a way for me to open the doors without a wife mark. My excitement ebbed away. I came back out of the barn and saw Vidar, his head drooping. The collar around his neck was so riddled with cracks, I could not imagine how it stayed in one piece.

I'm sorry.

"For what? Healing me?"

No. That, I will never regret. Never! I am sorry I wasn't brave enough to use this mark at the beginning.

"I didn't want to be your wife then. I'm not sure I want to be your wife now."

Vidar curled in on himself, coiling like a rope. *The mark binds me to you, not the other way around. From this day forward, my fate is tied to yours. My power and secrets are at your disposal. My very life depends on yours. But we have not married. You are as free to leave as you were yesterday.*

"What will happen to you if I do?"

I cannot say for sure. Unless you betray me to those who wish me harm, I suspect I would go on living to—

"Wait. Do you mean to say that my leaving might kill you?"

Not necessarily. There are stories of dragons who survive their mates leaving them.

"But some dragons die when the women they've wife-marked leave them?"

Well, yes, but in most of those cases, the women deliberately set out to destroy them. I don't think you would do that to me. Even if you did, I deserve to be punished for the way I've trapped you here.

I walked over to him and patted the warm, hard scales above his left foreleg, which was hanging down outside the coil. "You haven't trapped me here. Perhaps at the beginning, down in the cave, but even then, I think you were only giving me what I needed—shelter and food. A place to rest. You took in a woman without power or connections or land, and you gave her a home. That does not deserve death."

I made you my pet.

"What else could you have done? You couldn't trust a sacrifice from Sir Drake, and you are far too kind to leave me out on a hillside to die."

I should have been braver. Or smarter. I should have found a better way. I am sorry. A giant tear rolled, steaming, from his eye.

"I forgive you," I whispered and hugged his leg, which was as much of him as I could get my arms around. "And I don't think I want to go anywhere just now."

He shuddered, and more tears fell. I held him until the quaking stopped. Then I changed clothes, found some breakfast, and got to work in the gardens.

CHAPTER SIXTEEN

Lambing

he first of the lambs were born one night about a week after Vidar gave me the wife mark. The night was chilly, the stars as thick in the sky as daisies in the back meadow at home.

At first, I wasn't sure what had awakened me and drawn me out of the bunkhouse. I could see nothing amiss, hear nothing unusual, but I couldn't relax. Was Adramelech near again?

It's Little Lady. On the hill beyond the orchard.

The urgency in Vidar's thought had me running past the barn and through the path between the tiny saplings in their larger support cages.

When I got close, I could hear Little Lady bleating pitifully and the others answering in worried bleats of their own. I should have expected Lady to have some trouble—she was so small. But I had rarely been involved with the lambing—only sometimes caring for a young one afterward if the mother hadn't made it. Still, I knew the general idea and had twice assisted when too many ewes struggled with birthing at the same time.

"Settle down, everybody," I said. "Let's see what's wrong."

The sheep calmed and turned adoring faces toward me, which, strangely enough, heightened my anxiety. The poor beasts trusted me, and I barely had any idea what I was doing.

You will be fine. Vidar's thought came at me with a wave of calm.

"Vidar! What have I told you about forcing me to think and feel the way you want me to?"

Sorry. I didn't mean to. It's just…. You were so distressed, I couldn't help myself.

I shook my head. At least the spurt of anger had cleared my head. What would my father do next?

Wash his hands. Bother. I hadn't brought a bucket of water or soap or anything.

I will get them for you.

Vidar would get them? How? He couldn't fit through the bunkhouse or barn doors.

The same way I brought you out from the bunkhouse when you were so ill.

I hardly had any time to ponder that when I heard an odd whistling noise. I turned toward it and flinched when I saw a white flapping thing racing through the air toward me.

I will not let it hit you.

I opened my eyes and was able to distinguish that the white flapping thing was a towel. Next to it, a couple of dark smudges also careened toward me. I had only just managed to make out the shape of the larger one—a bucket—when it came to a sudden stop two feet from me, sloshing half its contents over the edge. Most of the water missed my nightgown.

I took in a deep breath. Next time I woke feeling that the sheep needed me, I'd collect a few basic supplies before rushing toward them. I scrubbed my hands and then approached the nether end of Little Lady. I did not look forward to what came next, but it had to be done.

Why?

"I need to figure out what the problem is, and the only way I know to do that is to reach inside."

Oh. I didn't realize. I don't think my father ever did that. There must be some magical way.

"If you don't happen to know what it is and how to do it right now, we're going to have to do this the human way." I know I sounded sharp, but I couldn't help it. It was the middle of the night, and I stood on a chilly hillside, trying to settle my nerves enough to remember what to do in a life and death situation that I'd only ever watched twice, the most recent time at least two years ago.

Little Lady bleated piteously. Poor girl. I moved behind her, took a deep breath, and wished I could see what I was doing better.

That, I can help with.

I felt more than heard Vidar puff out a great breath of air, and all the field around us glowed brightly, nearly as light as day. I glanced toward the light and saw a giant glowing bubble hanging in the air between Vidar and me.

"Thank you. That helps." I turned my attention back to Little Lady. No time like the present. I took a step closer, and she moved her hindquarters further away.

"Come on, girl. I want to help. I know it hurts, but you need to hold still."

I can hold her still. And maybe help with the pain, too. Vidar closed his eyes.

Little Lady's bleating stopped, and she shifted back towards me. I didn't have much practice interpreting sheep expressions, but she seemed happy.

I shook my head. It was almost frightening, the way Vidar could influence them. If he didn't mean them well—"

But I do mean them well. And that means you need to help her, doesn't it?

So, I did. I took another deep breath and eased my right hand in to see what was happening. Not that I could see, of course, but feeling around, I tried to make sense of what my hand touched. One hoof. Two hooves. Three hooves. That wasn't good. I shouldn't be able to feel the back hooves. A nose. Another nose. Wait. Was it another nose, or the first one?

There are definitely two. I can hear their surprise at something poking at them.

Of course, he could. By now, I'd found the fourth front hoof and had my arm crushed by Little Lady's body trying to expel the little creatures, and me as well. I grimaced.

I could help you with the pain.

"No!" I bit my lip and focused on not screaming as the grinding pain came again. When it let up, I felt around until I could tell which lamb was which. The two were terribly tangled together. They'd never make it out that way. I eased and separated, taking breaks only when the pain became too intense. Eventually, I managed to push one little creature back. Then I held the other's front hooves and tugged, pulling as gently as I could while still using my full strength.

At first, it seemed like nothing was happening, but then the tension shifted, and I staggered backward, falling on my rump with the bloody little lamb on my lap.

Before I could right myself, her brother was also born, and Little Lady turned to lick them off and prod them up onto their shaky legs.

I laughed to see them wobbling there, searching under their mother for their first drink. These two would do all right.

I smiled ruefully at my nightgown. It would take a lot of cleaning, as would the rest of me. I rubbed my bruised arm, surprised it didn't hurt more. It had been pulverized during the birthing.

Beneath the blood and gore, I could see dark bruises shifting to yellow and then back to normal skin color. "How is this happening?"

Dragonwives heal better and more quickly than normal humans. Not just from illness, but also from injury.

I gaped at my pain-free, no-longer-bruised arm. "I had no idea."

Few women would survive dragon births without the changes. Even the pet mark conveys some benefit.

"I got sick when I had that mark."

So you did.

I yawned. The lambs were adorable, but now that both they and their mother were doing well, nothing seemed so attractive as my bed. I scrubbed my arms and then tossed the rest of the water out over the hillside.

You didn't need the rest of the water for your clothing?

"I don't wash my clothes while I'm wearing them." I laughed. "Come on. So far as I can tell, they'll be all right until morning." I started back toward the bunkhouse.

I'll stay here. I was sleeping outside anyway. It won't hurt to keep my wary eye on our woolly friends.

Part of me wanted to stay with them all, but the rest of me wanted to lie down. I yawned again. Little Lady shuddered. I ran back toward her, worried that I'd missed something important. I reached her just as two shiny sacs of blood and tissue dropped to the grass. I'd forgotten the afterbirth. I turned away, not wanting to see the next part.

Why? What—ew! That's disgusting. Why does she do that?

"Papa always said that eating the afterbirth made the mothers healthier and kept the wolves from smelling that there are new lambs." I wrinkled my nose. "Maybe it does. Even so, I don't like to watch."

Me either. Vidar curled himself in a wide circle around the sheep and rested his head on his back haunches, facing outward. The sheep wouldn't need to worry about wolves tonight.

I smiled. "Goodnight, Vidar."

"Goodnight, my love." His smile showed more jagged teeth than made for comfort, but I felt the genuine caring that lay masked beneath the threat.

I nodded and returned to the bunkhouse. Morning was fast approaching before I'd managed to remove all the blood, mud, and grass stains from my nightgown, but I would sleep anyway. I waved a goodnight to the morning stars and crept into my bunk.

When I returned to the hillside pasture much later that morning, Vidar was watching the sheep with a bemused expression in his eyes. *I'd forgotten what it was like to watch baby animals in the spring. There's so much life in them. What do you think about Lightfoot and Beauty?*

"Lightfoot and Beauty?"

As names for the lambs.

I smiled and leaned up against his side to watch the antics of the little ones. "Perfect."

A sadness slipped over me, and it took me a bit to realize it was coming from Vidar. "What's wrong?"

If I love them, they'll be a target for Adramelech. I'm putting them in danger, much as I'm putting you in danger.

"I was already Adramelech's target, remember? I don't know why he wants me, but he said he did. You haven't put me in danger. You've protected me from it. Still, if there are ways to strengthen the farm's defenses and give our sheep a hope of living, I suppose we'd better discover what they are."

I nestled even closer to Vidar. "The next time that monster comes here, I want to be ready for him."

CHAPTER SEVENTEEN

Mind Games

idar thought we should wait until all the sheep had lambed before going down to Dragonhome to look for protective magic. He didn't want Fern, Blackie, or Dancer to need help while we were hours away, beneath the earth.

I agreed with him, though every time I thought about Adramelech approaching while the sheep still had little protection, it caused a tight pain in my chest. It wasn't that I wanted to bury myself under the mountain. I still preferred the open farm to the pearl-washed cavern under the ground. I did want the sheep to be safe, though, and none of the books we'd brought with us showed how to accomplish that.

The animal husbandry one did tell Vidar how to magically assist with a lambing, though, and I felt something akin to disappointment from him when Fern, Blackie, and Dancer all managed to birth their lambs without assistance.

I thought Dancer would need our help since she was also carrying twins. Vidar's lower jaw stuck out in a way that reminded me forcefully of my brother Lark when he was pouting.

I laughed at him.

I am not pouting.

"If you say so."

I am glad they did not need my help. But if I'd known we weren't needed, we could have gone to Dragonhome a week ago and been back already.

"No one can predict the future."

Of course, people can predict the future. I always know what the weather will be. A green dragon or an orange one would have been able to tell months ago when the lambs would drop and with how much trouble.

"Why green or orange?"

Just as black dragons are good with weather, green dragons grow things, and orange ones are good with beasts. Father made me learn all the colors once.

"What is purple for?"

Illusions. And sometimes power over humans.

"I thought all dragons had that."

Well, yes. Any dragon can do any magic, but we do some better than others. Our strengths often depend on our natural affinities, and those are connected to our color.

"So, my ability to keep you from compelling me to do things shows that your human-influencing enchantments are weak?"

I don't think so. You are also reclaiming your mind from Adramelech, and by all accounts, his is exceptionally strong.

From Adramelech? But it was Sir Drake who—

Gold chains flashed in my mind, and I fought them. A memory flickered across my inner eyelids—the first day I'd met Sir Drake and recognized his eyes, and he enspelled me. Because Sir Drake was Adramelech! I'd recognized him, and he couldn't let me go around telling everyone what I knew. He had hidden my knowledge even from myself. But now, as I fought the chains, I could see clearly. I understood what Vidar had said when I first arrived here— Sir Drake couldn't afford to destroy the dragon who had attacked my farm. Sir Drake, himself, was that dragon.

As soon as I recalled that first time I had recognized Sir Drake as Adramelech, more memories emerged—times when my knowledge rose to the surface, and Sir Drake had added new golden chains to block me from my memories. Dozens upon dozens of them had cluttered my mind, but now, every chain crumbled into a great heap of gold dust that blew away, as if a cleansing breeze had swept through, clearing all the rubbish away.

Vidar chuckled. *That had to hurt.*

Actually, I felt surprisingly good. No headache. For the first time in a long time, I felt like I knew myself.

I didn't mean it hurt you. I'm sure it hurt Adramelech when you broke through all those enchantments.

"Good." My mind sorted through memories that seemed new to me—many memories of recognizing Sir Drake and challenging him. Each time, he'd locked my memories from me and wiped the minds of the girls around me so that they turned from their momentary horror and reverted back to fawning devotion. "Why didn't he just kill me?"

That, my Rilla, is a very good question indeed. Perhaps he felt the need to challenge himself, though that would be unusual for him. Perhaps he feels killing you would mean admitting defeat.

"He hates to lose anything."

Yes, I believe that is the case. Perhaps it is none of those reasons, though. It may be worthwhile for you to search your newly uncovered memories for some indications of his thoughts. I have always found with Adramelech that what I do not know can definitely hurt me.

"I will try. Perhaps while we travel back." Thinking of Adramelech had me wanting to shore up our defenses sooner rather than later.

Vidar nodded, and we readied for the trip.

But as much as I combed my memories on the walk-fly to the cavern, I could not puzzle out what Sir Drake was about. He treated me differently from the other girls—never striking me or humiliating me, either in private or in front of the others, though I'd often seen him strike Bria—that was the name of the girl who'd been wearing white in my first memory of the palace.

I suspected he'd done worse when she attended him behind closed doors. Bria often wore long sleeves, and unfashionably high necklines, and flinched if someone accidentally brushed her arm or side. I'd asked her once about it and urged her to write to her parents if the magician was abusing her, and she'd assured me that she loved the time she spent serving Sir Drake.

"Besides," she'd said, her smile slipping a bit. "I once wrote home, and my parents told me that this was the best place for me."

"Did you tell them Sir Drake strikes you?"

"Oh, but Sir Drake doesn't strike me any more than my father and brothers did when I was home. It's nothing. Really. In fact, Sir Drake is much better than they were, for he never whips me unless I ask him to."

"You ask him to whip you? Why would you do that?"

"I should be whipped if I have done wrong. And I'm always doing things wrong. I break things and rip things. I don't mean to, but I'm so clumsy."

"You're never clumsy when you're with me or the other girls and Sir Drake isn't with us. And you don't deserve to be whipped if you accidentally break something around Sir Drake."

"I also steal things," Bria whispered. "I never used to, but now I can't help myself. I see something bright and shiny, and I can't help taking it. When Sir Drake catches me, if I beg him, he punishes me himself instead of reporting the theft to the guards. I couldn't stand to be banished to Arkon."

"We don't banish people to Arkon for theft," I said.

"When you steal the king's rubies, they do."

"You stole—"

"No! I mean, I must have because they were in my reticule after the last garden party where he wore them, but I distinctly remember seeing them, and wanting to, and then helping bring up all those bottles of wine from the cellar, so

I wouldn't have the chance to give in to temptation. I had been doing so well, too. I hadn't stolen anything in weeks." Bria broke down and sobbed.

I started to pat her back, but then remembered she'd been whipped. I settled for setting a light hand on her shoulder and keeping my troubled thoughts to myself. I didn't know exactly what was happening, but I suspected that somehow Sir Drake was manipulating events so that he could torture this girl—the kindest of the girls I'd met at the palace. Had he used magic to plant the rubies in Bria's reticule? Now, in retrospect, I was sure of it. In fact, he had likely compelled her to steal as well, since she had never done so before coming to the palace. And when her sense of self-preservation finally overcame the compulsion to steal that he'd created in her, he found a way to make her believe she had done the crime anyway.

Knowing that Sir Drake was actually Adramelech made it plain why all those girls in the palace had seemed so strangely attracted to him, even though he mistreated them. They were not themselves. I wondered what Alvina, Bria, and Kali had been like before they met Sir Drake.

None of this helped me understand what Sir Drake wanted with me, though.

Doesn't it?

"No! Why? What do you understand that I have not seen?"

We know that Adramelech takes pleasure in the pain of others, but your friend's story suggests that he also gains pleasure from bending a woman's will until she inflicts the pain on herself.

"Yes, but I've never wanted to do that."

No. He has not yet been able to break you. Which makes me think his desire to do so has only increased. Whatever plan he has for me, it involves making you bend to his will.

"I will never bow to him!"

I have hope that you are strong enough to avoid doing so.

The way Vidar looked at me made my face heat.

I have already told you I love you. I will do whatever necessary to keep you safe.

It always made me slightly uncomfortable when Vidar said he loved me, but his promise to keep me safe comforted me. I didn't know how much he could do against Adramelech with the collar still on, but that fetter had so many cracks already, surely it would completely break soon.

And when it does, I will end him. That spell I have long known how to do.

"Your father taught you how to kill another dragon?"

No. I learned that spell when Adramelech used it to kill my father.

"Will using one of Adramelech's spells change the kind of person you are?"

He deserves it!

"I didn't say he didn't."

Vidar withdrew himself from my mind then, and I found myself wondering what he was thinking. It wasn't fair—the way he could walk in and out of my mind, but I could only see the glimpses he wanted to show me of his. I imagined a wall around my own thoughts that kept them private.

At my side, Vidar stumbled, crashing to the tunnel floor. I jerked out of his way. "Vidar! Vidar! What's wrong? Speak to me, please!"

From his lips instead of his mind came a strange, hissing, semblance of language. "Mss kk nnn."

"Mss kk nn? Must? Must something nn—in?"

Vidar nodded. "Mss...nn."

Must in? Was that it?

I remembered the wall I had imagined in my mind and let it crumble into rubble.

Thank you. Vidar rose shakily to his feet. *Now that we are bonded, I cannot bear to be cut off from you.*

"Does that mean you cannot travel beyond the range where you can hear my thoughts?"

I do not know, but I don't think so. My father would often travel to the border without my mother, and it did not trouble me when I was hunting or pursuing Adramelech. I am only undone when you shut me out yourself.

"Then I will try not to, though I still think it is unfair for you to know my thoughts when I cannot know yours."

Perhaps you can. We will look for that also in the library.

"I didn't think women could do magic."

Who told you that?

Sir Drake, of course. I felt stupid. I'm not sure why I'd ever believed anything he said, but I suppose since he was the only magician I'd ever met, I'd assumed he knew what he was speaking of. Though even when I thought him human, I'd known he was as likely to lie as to speak truth.

My father said that magic comes with dragon blood, and also with the claiming marks, so you can do it now, even if you could not before.

"How could I have done it before? I am no dragon."

My love, every child of a dragon carries dragon blood, even the dragondaughters. Many a child of dragons has gone out into the world and mixed with humans. Nearly anyone could have a bit of the blood. But I shouldn't think Adramelech would want his playthings to make use of such powers, even if he is attracted to women who have them. A woman too strong in the blood might well find ways to evade his traps.

As I had done. Again and again.

Indeed. I imagine he lied to you because he knew that if you had such powers and learned how to use them, you might even be able to destroy him. No smart dragon underestimates an enchantress.

"Is Adramelech a smart dragon?"

I am beginning to wonder.

CHAPTER EIGHTEEN

The Magic Library

he library in Dragonhome had transformed. A giant textured map covered the formerly blank wall behind the large desk. It was clearly magical, for tiny figures moved upon it. I pressed close to the basin that represented the farm and could make out the tiny shapes of all twelve of our sheep, gamboling in a field by the river. I smiled.

If you press the dragon symbol on Dragonhome mountain, it should open the case of magical books.

"The symbol that represents you? Does that mean this case cannot be opened unless you are here?"

No, not the one that represents me. The one drawn in gold.

I saw it then, cleverly twining through the mountains around the farm. It was the first gold dragon I had seen among all the dragon artwork in Dragonhome.

We are proud of our black, but sometimes it is good to remember that most of the strongest dragons are gold.

"Why?"

Gold dragons are gifted at magic that affects other dragons, so they are often our leaders, and the ones who are most battle-tested. Though now and again other colors rise to the top. We respect old dragons of any color.

"How old, exactly, does a dragon have to be for you to think he's old?" I asked as I put a hand to the gold dragon in the mountain. The texture of the map tickled my palm.

Anyone who has seen more than a thousand summers is old by my reckoning. As he spoke, the map in front of me cracked down the center.

I don't know whether it was the wall or Vidar's answer that shocked me more, but it was the former that had me staggering away from the map, fearing I'd broken it. The two sections slid away from each other to the right and left, revealing a marble bookcase full of the oldest books I had yet seen. I was almost afraid to touch them.

There are gloves you can use in the desk.

I found them in the second drawer on the left—beautiful white gloves that seemed made just for me, so closely did they fit. I turned back to the bookshelf. "Is there something in particular I should be looking for?"

I remember a large, red-bound volume and a small white one that might help.

As I scanned the bookcase, my eyes lit on at least four large red volumes and a dozen small white ones.

Perhaps we should start with the red.

"Agreed. But if we need to read all of them, this will take months." I pulled the first red one off the shelf and heard a noise I didn't understand. I swirled to face the disturbance and found that a doorway had covered the archway to the library. There was no way out.

I'd forgotten about the door.

"What about the door? Will I be stuck in here?" My heart beat quickly in my throat, and a band of fear squeezed my chest.

No. The archway will clear again when you put the book back. It was Father's way of making sure that all his books stayed in his library.

"You're sure?"

Very sure. The books on that case were never meant to be taken from this room, and this way Father ensured that neither he nor anyone else wandered about with them. You see, my father was apt to walk about while reading, and he often left books all through the house. Mother was constantly returning stacks of them to the library, but sometimes it took a few days. Father didn't want the books on the magic shelf to be out where just anyone could reach them for even that long. He was always worried they would find their way to the wrong hands.

"Had that ever happened?"

I think it must have from the way he warned us against the problem, but he never told me the story.

I glanced nervously at the door. I hated feeling trapped.

I am sorry, my Rilla. I truly had forgotten my father's charm to keep the magic books in one place. It never bothered me the way it does you.

I took deep breaths to calm my racing heart. "I can do what I must to protect our sheep and our farm." I set the large red book on the desk and leafed through it. Nearly every page had illustrations with odd geometric shapes in a variety of colors and combinations. Unfamiliar words explained what appeared to be recipes, but with metals and earth instead of food. Unless dragons could eat stone?

I didn't know Father had an alchemy book. I wonder what he used it for? I never knew him to practice the odiferous art.

"So, this isn't the book you were looking for?"

I'm afraid not.

At least we hadn't needed to read the whole thing before discovering that. I turned back to the bookshelf and tried to pull out one of the other large red volumes, but it was stuck in place, as if cemented to the case. I tried another, and it was stuck as well. In fact, every book in the case seemed locked there. I was surprised I'd gotten the first one out so easily.

The bookshelf may only allow one book to be read at a time. If you put the alchemy book back, can you access the others?

I tried it. With the alchemy book back in its place (and the bookcase blocked me from setting it in any free space but its own), the ones beside it loosened, and I heard a sound behind me. I turned to see that the doorway had reopened, which relieved me. It wasn't that I distrusted

Vidar, but that locked doors made me nervous. I turned back to the bookshelf and tried, just for experimentation's sake, to pull both of the next two red books out at the same time, but they locked in place before I'd half removed them.

Father was almost as protective of his library as he was of his family. He always said that we must be very careful with it because evil people could use it to do great damage.

I could see why. Though all books were wonderful, the ones beneath my fingers radiated power—and I'd barely opened even one of them. If Adramelech could read these, he might increase his power beyond all reason. On the other hand, if ordinary people who had a hint of dragon blood were able to see them, perhaps they could learn to defend themselves. Perhaps someone like my father would have had more than a hoe in his hand when he met Adramelech.

I'd never thought of it that way. I am not sure what is best. I know my father felt that knowledge was dangerous in the wrong hands.

Perhaps it was. But who got to decide which were the right hands? Vidar's father alone? The king? (He apparently trusted Sir Drake—and wasn't that a nightmare?)

Do you think the king trusts Sir Drake? Or is the king in thrall to him?

I chose a second large red book to take back to the desk as I thought about Vidar's question. My recently returned memories told me that I'd met the king when I was at the palace, but though I sifted through that whole section of my past, I could not recall a single time when I had conversed with him or even overheard him conversing with others naturally.

On the other hand, the way he looked at Sir Drake had triggered at least two occasions when I recognized the connection between the magician and the dragon. I was sure the king knew Sir Drake and the dragon had some kind of connection, but I was less sure that the king fully understood what that connection was. Was the king aware that his chief adviser was, in fact, a dragon? I'd never been around the man enough to be certain how much he really knew.

I shouldn't think Adramelech wanted you around the king much if the man's visage helped you recognize Sir Drake for what he was.

"I'm sure that's true. The other girls also thought Sir Drake was trying to keep me to himself, and they seemed to understand him as well as anyone." I opened the book in front of me and stared, paralyzed, as fire licked up at me from the illustrations.

Not that one, Rilla!

CHAPTER NINETEEN

𝔚𝔞𝔩𝔩𝔰

 wasn't sure why Vidar sounded so panicked until the fire lit the finger of one of my gloves. I slammed the book shut and grabbed the lit finger with the other hand to smother the flame. Once it was out, I couldn't help staring at the charred holes in the gloves and my blistered skin beneath them. That was going to hurt for a while.

Not so very long, I hope. Dragonwives heal very quickly from fire damage.

Even as he spoke, the burned flesh smoothed and healed over. The gloves, however, would require repairs, and I doubted they would ever again be useful for handling books.

I may be able to fix that. Minor repairs don't take much magic, and I learned to restore burned fabric when I was still very young.

"You mended your own clothes?"

If I burned it, I fixed it. Those were my parents' rules. I burned a great many things when I was first coming into my fire.

As I stared at my gloves, the black edges around the holes got lighter and lighter until they were as white as the rest of the glove. The holes grew together, much as my skin had. In moments there was no way to tell the mending from the original gloves.

Excellent. I may sleep a bit now. That took more magic than I remembered. Vidar's voice cut off abruptly.

"Vidar? Vidar!? I rushed toward the door, forgetting that it was shut. Cursing, I ran back to the desk, returned the book to its case, and sprinted back toward the entrance, which was now clear of any obstruction. I dashed through Dragonhome, even crawling quickly when I got to the entrance tunnel, which was half blocked by Vidar, who had coiled himself upon the ground before the doorway. He'd been careful to leave enough room above him that I could have climbed over him if I'd needed to, which scared me more than his thoughts stopping. Was he worried about dying?

Rilla? Is something wrong? You feel frightened.

"You stopped thinking at me so suddenly that I needed to see that you were all right."

Oh, yes. I think so. Just tired. Sorry to have left you to work on your own.

I could feel the exhaustion pouring off him now and wondered how I'd missed it before. Why would repairing the gloves wear him out so much when all the mists and glassmaking had not?

Creating material is always more difficult than changing material that is already made. And weather magic is my specialty. But do not worry. I am only a bit tired. I will be fine after a rest.

"Well, that's fine then. Just checking. I'll get back to work." I crept backward and then tiptoed to the library, though I couldn't entirely quiet my thoughts. Perhaps he was tired enough not to be bothered by them, though.

The magical bookcase had closed while I went to see Vidar, but it was simple to open it again. I took out the third red book. Should I open it? What if it contained something like the fire of the last book? Vidar wasn't awake to help me. Though did he need to be? He claimed that even in sleep, half his mind still watched for trouble. He'd certainly answered when I went to see if he had suffered serious damage.

Gingerly I opened the book. Nothing emerged from the pages. In fact, there were no illustrations, only words in some foreign tongue with an elegant but indecipherable script. If this was the book we needed, we were in serious trouble, for I couldn't read it, and I couldn't take it out to Vidar for him to read either.

I replaced the book in the bookshelf and tried the fourth book. Like the last, this one held only words, but at least they were words I could understand. Within a short time, I was convinced this was the book we wanted. It gave instructions on shielding lands, homes, people, animals, and treasure. One section explained how to make things hard to find. There were mazes and camouflage, invisibility spells and enchantments that kept people from noticing things, even if they were in plain sight.

Next came a section of shields that protected against all kinds of physical attacks—poisons, fire, weapons, even being crushed. There were shields that could lessen or eliminate the damage caused by being immersed in water or other liquids. Others prevented lands, people, or things from becoming too hot or too cold. Still others warded against rocks—or even whole avalanches—falling from the sky.

If Vidar's father had known how to hide and defend Dragonhome, why was it not better protected when Adramelech's attack came. Or had all these many enchantments failed in the face of Adramelech's wrath?

A shiver snaked up my spine. I did not like living here beneath the earth, but I had imagined myself safe here.

And perhaps I was. Had not Dragonhome remained untouched in all the long years since Adramelech's attack?

Idly, I flipped through to the next section, which discussed the building of walls and fortresses. This section was worn and often annotated in the hand I recognized from Vidar's father's journal. So, Vidar's father had put his faith in walls. Perhaps I needn't wait until Vidar awoke to understand what had made the farm vulnerable. I turned back to the beginning of the section and began anew, reading closely and paying special attention to the scribbles in the margins.

The going was slow at first, as I struggled to make sense of the old dragon's crabbed handwriting, but in time, I pieced together the pattern—Vidar's father had one great work. It was a wall on which he spent all his energy and time. The wall encircled our Heshal and The Wilds west of the Sicvan mountains. It even went through the sea, making a complete loop that separated us from Arkon. The notations in the book were hard for me to picture, but on the map, I could see the walls as a strong black line that enclosed the territory with magic so powerful that in a thousand years, none but Adramelech had breached it.

CHAPTER TWENTY

𝔅reaches

*e did not breach it, exactly*

"You're up!"

Yes. I don't need long to replenish my energy. I see you've found the right book.

"Why didn't your father protect the farm better?"

All magic comes at a price, my Rilla. Even the most powerful of dragons cannot sustain every spell at the same time. My father felt that after Dragonhome, the wall was the most important, for it kept out the evils of Arkon and the ocean kingdoms. He imagined that in the case of any assault, there would be time to get the family down to Dragonhome. Even a dragon cannot get from the wall to here instantly. And we all would feel if the wall were breached.

"Then how—"

My brother thought Adramelech was a friend and brought him through. He only realized his mistake when Adramelech razed the farm, but by then it was too late.

"What happened to your brother?"

He died defending my mother. Probably just as well. I was so angry at him in that moment that if Adramelech had not killed him, I might have tried to do it myself—and I don't know if I could have lived with myself after doing such a thing.

I gasped. I couldn't imagine how it would feel to be betrayed by my own family that way.

In the beginning I felt betrayed, but over the years, as I've watched Adramelech deceive, manipulate, and control the people around him, I've come to suspect that my brother had no idea who he was bringing through the wall. He was the most shocked of any of us when Adramelech attacked.

I sifted back through my memories of Sir Drake at the palace, and I had to admit Vidar was right. Sir Drake rarely attacked directly, and frequently posed as someone's friend while undermining their interests or simultaneously supporting their opponents. It was a wonder any in the palace let him near them at all.

Most of the courtiers lack your ability to fight off his mind games, and many of them owe their positions to him, so they cannot complain too loudly—what a dragon has given, he can as easily take away. I suspect, though, that ill will toward him has been rising, or he would not have attacked your farm.

"I don't understand. How does that help him avoid ill will?"

It makes him indispensable. Who but Sir Drake stands a chance against a dragon?

"But he can't fight himself!"

Of course not. I suspect that is why he is now attacking me more actively again. It is probably also one of the reasons why you were sent to me. He may have other plans for you, but for the moment, he needs you somewhere away from the court. He cannot afford to have any of his detractors discover the truth about him just now. He might be run out of Heshal as surely as he was run out of Arkon.

"He was run out of Arkon? Did he cause too many fights there, too?"

In a manner of speaking. He convinced two of the younger princes to threaten their father for the throne. Renove was forced to kill them both, and the battle left him weakened. Before any of his court officials could take advantage of that weakness, he had them executed for supporting his sons or sent off on suicide missions to prove their loyalty to the crown.

"Adramelech escaped instead?"

No. Defeating my father and breaking open the wall to allow Arkon to invade was his suicide mission.

"But he is too frightened to return?"

He has not yet accomplished the mission. My father's wall still stands. It may even be stronger with my tending than it was when Adramelech first ambushed us.

I turned to the map on the wall behind the desk and traced the line that had protected my country without any of us ever knowing about it. As I skimmed down the mountains to the west, I noticed dozens upon dozens of tiny dragon symbols clumped near one of the tallest mountains. "Are there always so many dragons massed on the Arkon side?" I asked.

There are always a few. I can usually feel them. I can sense five there now.

"Vidar, the map shows closer to a hundred. All at the mountain marked with an eagle."

Clear Eye Pass. They mean to break through. I wonder how they are shielding their presence. Thank goodness you've seen them. Little one, I must stop them, but I haven't the power to work the magic from here. Please, lock the doors and open them to no one until I return and tell you it is safe.

"But Vidar—"

Please, Rilla. I know you don't like it here, but it would kill me if you died.

"Vidar, don't be ridiculous. You survived losing all your family, and you barely know me."

But I've bonded to you. My heart is now tied to yours. When you die, so shall I. It is always this way with dragons. How else would a sniveling weakling like Adramelech ever have destroyed my father? He merely distracted the man, and then ambushed my mother and the others. When my father raced back and found my mother dead, he could barely stand, let alone fight. And once Father was gone, my brothers were too angry with each other to work together well. Adramelech found them easy prey. I still am surprised I survived.

I took a deep breath. I could hardly believe what I was about to say. "I understand why you must go, and I'll stay down here with the door locked until you come for me. But Vidar?"

Yes, my love?

"If…If Adramelech somehow gets through anyway, you must promise me to stay alive and strong at least long enough to end him."

Rilla, if my father could not—

"You are not your father!"

Dejection spilled from him, filling Dragonhome.

"You are stronger! You have survived death, hopelessness, and bondage, and still, you find the strength to do your duty. You are larger than Adramelech and strong in magic, even with the collar on. You can promise me this."

I felt hope rise in him, clearing away the clouds of depression. *I promise. Though it be impossible, still I will do it. I love you, my Rilla.*

"Let me say goodbye to you," I said.

He seemed confused as I put the book away and came out to the cavern of Dragonhome. *We were already saying goodbye.*

I reached up and stroked his snout. "In person is better."

Sadness washed over me, and I was surprised to find it was my own. "Be careful."

Always.

"Is there anything I can do to protect the orchard and sheep myself?"

I am not sure. Magic is not mastered in a moment. Look for the book called First Steps. *And if you read me the shield of disinterest as I am going out of the cavern, I can do that one before I go. If I recall, it takes little magic and less time, but may well keep them out of Adramelech's eye.*

"I will do that."

I must go. The attack on the wall could come at any time.

"Go," I said, "but return to me soon."

Lock the door behind me. He flew, soaring through the cavern toward the opposite end, as if afraid he would not leave if he lingered any longer.

I watched him until he landed and squeezed into one of the tunnels. Then I crept back inside, shutting myself in. *I do this of my own free will,* I reminded myself, but the walls still seemed to press in, the mountains above me to press down. I could leave if I needed to this time. I pressed my hand against the door, and watched it swing open again, just to be sure.

Then I resealed it, returned to the library, found the spell Vidar needed for the sheep, and read it to him three times in a row. I checked his accuracy as he recited the instructions back to me and listened in as he performed the spell over the sheep.

Goodbye, my love. I must now fly like the wind.

"Be careful," I said.

You, too. I love you.

And then I heard him no more, though I could track his dragon symbol crossing the map, moving surprisingly slowly for one who said he would fly like the wind. Though, I supposed even the wind took time to travel all that distance.

When I tired of watching the tiny dragon symbol creep across the map, I put the magic book away, left the library, sat before the fire, and let myself cry. My mother would have scolded me for crying when I was warm and safe and well fed, but she wasn't here.

Nor was anyone else.

I was alone again, buried beneath the earth, and though he had not said as much, the only one who knew how to find me was flying into danger.

CHAPTER TWENTY-ONE
Unwelcome Thoughts

 would go stir-crazy in this glorified crypt if I didn't do something beyond eat, sleep, and watch Vidar's tiny black dragon symbol make slow progress across the map toward Clear Eye, so I opened the magic library and looked for the book Vidar had mentioned.

It was surprisingly easy to find, for unlike the other books, *First Steps* had its title stamped on the spine. It looked even older than the others, with dog-eared pages and a binding so loose, I feared the insides might shake free. I supposed that was what happened to a book when it was used by generations of young dragons and their sisters.

Were the sisters taught with the brothers as I'd learned alongside Khan and Lark? Or did Vidar's father agree with the village elders who said it was a mistake to educate women? Vidar's surprise at my knowing how to read made it rather more likely than not that his sisters hadn't been taught even the rudiments of an education, let alone magic.

I felt unreasonably grumpy with Vidar's father, though I couldn't be sure I had cause, and it wouldn't do any good anyway. After all, the man had died centuries before I was even thought of. I don't know why it bothered me—the way the old dragon had hoarded his knowledge. That was what dragons did after all, wasn't it? They hoarded treasure. Not that I'd ever before heard of a dragon who hoarded books. It was always gold or silver or precious stones.

Or women. An unwelcome voice slipped into my head. *A good many of us hoard women as well.*

"Adramelech," I breathed. Where was he? I swung toward the map and saw a tiny purple dragon over the farm. "No—no—no!"

I couldn't let him see into my mind—see the things I wanted protected.

Oh, my sweet. I would never hurt anything important to you.

Was he out of his mind? Did he think I couldn't recall what he'd done at my farm?

You shouldn't be able to— his thoughts cut off as if a wall had slammed down.

I shouldn't be able to what? Remember who he was and all he had done to me? Because he'd put those golden chains in my mind? And was likely to do so again. But perhaps I could cut him off, the way I had cut off Vidar that once?

You blocked out Vidar? I'd have liked to see that. Did it stop his heart, the poor wee thing?

"Get out of my mind!" I shouted, imagining myself pushing at Sir Drake with a spear until he stumbled backward, bleeding a bit. As soon as it felt as if he'd cleared my mind, I dreamed up thick brick walls between us, fencing me all about. No, not brick. Too weak. Stone, thick as mountains, with metal woven into the core.

An intense pain pressed against my skull on all sides, but I could not hear Adramelech any longer. I watched him on the map, prowling from one edge of the farm to another. I was relieved to see that the tiny barns and greenhouse retained their shape as he passed them instead of becoming lumpy ruins like the vineyard. Neither did Adramelech appear to notice the sheep, but rather he paced the edge of the basin where the entrance to the path to Dragonhome could be found. I held my breath, which did nothing for my aching head, and prayed he would not find what he sought.

For hours it seemed I waited there, barely daring to breathe, my head pounding from an external assault. I watched him pace. Back and forth. Now and again, he darted forward as if he saw something of interest, and each time, I gasped, then let the breath out slowly again when it was clear he had not found the way in.

At last the purple figure on the map stopped moving. The assault on my head eased. Then Adramelech's symbol took off after Vidar's, though how the older dragon hoped to catch up, I didn't know. Vidar flew much faster.

All the same, I wished I could warn Vidar that he now had enemies both behind and in front. Perhaps I still could. I turned back to the *First Steps* book and tried to flip through the pages to see if it had anything about communication magic, but the pages wouldn't turn. A large red line of text flashed:

Always Master The First Lesson Before Moving To the Second

Bossy little book, but as I'd never tried magic before, I supposed I ought to pay attention. What did I know? Perhaps it was best to do as the book said. I glanced back at the map. Vidar would be flying for many hours yet, judging by his progress across the map so far, and the distance between him and Adramelech was widening, not shrinking. I could study a little in hopes of learning something that might help in time. Either I would reach a lesson that taught something useful for warning Vidar, or I wouldn't, but if I did nothing, I had no hope of communicating with him at all.

I tamped down on my impatience and started at the top of the left-hand page.

Lesson One

Basics of Magic

CHAPTER TWENTY-TWO

Magic Lessons

 read the instructions slowly and carefully to make sure I wasn't missing anything.

Then I read them again, sure I was missing something. How could this be magic? It was mere breathing. In, hold, out, hold, repeat. What kind of nonsense was this? I wanted to help Vidar, not sit here wasting my time breathing! I knew how to breathe!

But the right-hand page wouldn't turn. The warning to take lessons in order flashed again. How could the book possibly know I wasn't taking the first lesson seriously?

The word magic in "Basics of Magic" grew larger and sparkled. Oh, fine then. So, this book was magical. Did that mean I had to do silly breathing exercises without any explanation of what they were good for? Apparently, I did, for the book refused to let me read any farther.

I sighed, pulled the book toward me, and tried the exercise. In-hold-out-hold.

Not enough to allow the right-hand page to turn.

I tried breathing this odd way for a full minute.

Still not enough.

Ten minutes by the great grandfather clock in the corner of the library was also too short. Anger built in my chest, but it was hard to hang onto when I was focused on my breathing. I let the anger go. I let all feelings go as I thought only of breathing. In-hold-out-hold. In-hold-out-hold.

I'd been sitting there, breathing, for about an hour when the right-hand page flapped open, and I was on to Lesson Two, which turned out to be nearly as disappointing as Lesson One. Instead of anything magical, this lesson had me dipping through my memories for things I'd long forgotten. Lesson Three felt like a language game, all rhymes and creaking puns. Lessons Four, Five, Six, and Seven were mere mathematics. Lesson Eight showed two nearly identical pictures, and I had to find all the differences between them. I considered giving up at that point, but my map showed Adramelech inexplicably gaining on Vidar. I wondered how this was possible when he'd been so much slower before. Whatever he was doing to catch up, I had to find a way to warn Vidar. I took a break in the main room to grab snacks and then returned to the library for more *First Steps*.

Lesson Nine was a long one. It taught me to identify hundreds of plants and what their various uses were for food, medicine, and magic. At least this lesson mentioned magic, though it didn't have me doing any yet.

Lesson Ten finally held something that I could see using, though not at the moment. It taught me how to use a dragon mark to call for help. It would come in handy if I were in immediate danger. I wasn't, though. Vidar was.

Fortunately, to pass this lesson, I did not have to send out an actual distress call, I only had to recite the instructions for doing so.

Lesson Eleven would send a warning. I read it as quickly as I could, and then tried it.

The force of the spell knocked me to my knees, and my head hurt. I desperately hoped it had worked, for I didn't think I could do it again. In fact, I thought I ought to stop for the night.

I rose shakily to my feet, picked up the *First Steps* book and turned toward the map.

Sinuous black writing next to Vidar's symbol said, "Thank you, my Rilla. Can you tell me more?"

I wished I could, but I had no idea how.

The words on the map disappeared and were replaced by new ones. "Use the black feather pen from the lower right-hand drawer to write on the map."

He hadn't wanted to mention this before he left? I found the pen he wrote about. There was no ink, so I tried to write on the map without any.

"Adramelech is chasing you, catching up," I wrote—at least I thought I did. The pen made no mark.

The writing on the map dissolved away, and new words replaced it. "Thank you again, my Rilla. I will be ready for him."

Vidar's symbol on the map picked up speed, and the distance between him and Adramelech widened again.

I slowly let out a breath I hadn't realized I was holding. Too exhausted to do anything else, I sank into the desk chair and slept.

When I awoke hours later with a crick in my neck, Vidar's symbol had made it two-thirds of the way to the mountains, and Adramelech was far behind. Since I still felt tired, I found *First Steps* where it had tumbled to the floor, returned it to its space in the bookshelf, and went out to the main part of Dragonhome for a meal, a bath, and a real rest.

CHAPTER TWENTY-THREE

Waiting

One of the things I hated about Dragonhome was waking alone in the dark, not knowing what time it was, or even what day. The blackness pressed in upon me, like the weight of a full mountain bearing down upon my chest.

I scrabbled around the floor above my head until I located the spot that turned on the light and I could see myself, a small human with hands that had seen far more labor than magic, trapped in a boudoir designed for dragons.

Well, not trapped. Vidar had given me the wife mark that would allow me to leave Dragonhome. If I needed to, I could find a way to navigate through the caverns and tunnels beneath the mountain and make my way back to the surface.

The pressure on my chest eased. I wondered how long I'd slept and if Vidar had already made his way to the border. Suddenly in a hurry, I saw to my urgent needs and rushed to the library to check the map.

Vidar's symbol was now more than three-quarters of the way there, with Adramelech's symbol trailing behind. I stared at the barely moving figures for several long minutes before deciding the map would probably not tell me anything new anytime soon—and even if it did, what good would such news do me or anyone?

Shaking my head at my own foolishness, I returned to the bedroom to dress in fresh clothes, straighten the blankets, and put the room to rights. I debated making bread but decided against it. I didn't want to be in the kitchen when Vidar reached the wall. Not that there was a thing I could do to help him when he did. I ate a bit of bread and cheese and returned to the library. Watching the map made my body feel tight, as if I were readying myself for a race. Not watching the map felt impossible.

To distract myself, I pulled *First Steps* from the magical bookcase and began again where I'd left off. But though I read the instructions for the next lesson—something about extending my hearing—I could not do it. Had I already reached my full magical capacity? I felt oddly disappointed, given that I'd never desired to become a magic practitioner. What did it matter whether I could become proficient at magic?

Except that if I mastered more magic, I could help protect the farm, and maybe defend myself if somehow Vidar—

But no, I didn't want to think about anything evil happening to Vidar.

I bit my lip and forced my mind back to the lesson. This time, as I followed the instructions, I found myself listening first to the tick of the grandfather clock, then to the crackle of fire in the main room, and then to the drip of water in the outer cavern of Dragonhome. I pushed the hearing further. Water trickled over rocks, and wind moaned in caverns like a lost animal calling out for its mother. Had Vidar moaned like that alone in these caves after his parents died?

With that, my extended hearing crumbled. Nothing came to my ears but the tick of the grandfather clock. Apparently, this magic took deep concentration. My eyes flitted to the map. I wasn't sure I could manage even partial concentration at the moment. I returned the magic primer to the shelf and looked about for a less demanding book to occupy my mind while I waited, but even non-magical books couldn't hold my attention for long. I found myself reading the same pages again and again without absorbing an iota of meaning.

Defeated, I returned to the main room for long enough to grab the knitting basket. This I could do while watching the map.

The wool slid softly through my fingers, and the needles clacked soothingly as I stared at the symbols that moved only slightly.

I hated waiting almost as much as I hated living in the heart of a mountain.

CHAPTER TWENTY-FOUR

Clear Eye

By the time Vidar reached the wall, I had knit nearly two handsbreadths up from the bottom of a sweater wide enough for a man bigger even than my father had been. I am not at all sure what possessed me to make something of that size, but it felt right to me, so I did it.

When Vidar reached the border, though, I set the sweater down and moved closer to the map. At first, I could not tell what Vidar was doing, but then, I noticed the wall changing near him. The line of wall that circled the country remained as thin as always in most places. Right in front of Vidar, though, the wall was thicker, and that thickness was spreading along the wall in both directions. The growth seemed slow, but I soon realized it crested mountains in moments.

I traced the thickening line, smiling to myself. This would keep those invaders out. I wished I could help somehow. I leaned in and prayed that Vidar would have the strength he needed and the time to finish.

Though why the Creator should listen to me, I had no idea. Certainly, he had not done anything when Adramelech attacked our farm. Nor had he intervened when Adramelech, masquerading as Sir Drake, locked me away in the palace and played around in my head. I didn't know why I called on the Creator now. Surely, he'd shown he cared nothing for me.

But what else could I do? I had discovered how to warn Vidar of impending doom, but Vidar already knew that Adramelech flew behind him. Undoubtedly Vidar was strengthening the wall as quickly as he possibly could.

I wondered if he would be finished before Adramelech reached him. Just glancing at the map made it seem a near thing. I used the grandfather clock's ceaseless ticking and the math I'd been recently reminded of to do a more accurate calculation.

Adramelech would reach Vidar in about two hours, and the wall would be finished about the same time. I located the pen Vidar had told me about the night before and wrote on the map, "Can you speed up at all? Adramelech will arrive near the time you finish."

"I will try," wrote Vidar.

"Can I help?"

"Not unless you wish to commit to me the way I have committed to you."

"You mean, become your real wife? How would that help?"

"It adds your strength to my own and allows you to carry the key to the wall and the new strengthening spell if I am unable to."

"Why would you be unable to?"

"If I am too injured to concentrate—or if I am dead."

I wanted to ask more about this. I wanted more time to think. This was too much, too fast. But even more than I wanted to be sure of myself, I wanted to keep those Adramelech-allied dragons out of the land of my birth, which I still loved, even if our king had teamed up with a monster. "What would I need to do?"

"I will write the incantation here. If you wish to do this, place your right hand on my mark and say it."

"I will," I wrote.

The words came through in a language I could not recognize, but somehow, I knew how to say them. I knew, also, roughly what they meant. I was putting my magic, my body, and my very life, at Vidar's disposal.

It was too much. How could I give all that?

Adramelech's symbol on the map accelerated.

I ran my calculations again. Adramelech would reach Vidar at least half an hour before the wall was complete. I couldn't let that happen.

I placed my right hand on Vidar's mark, directly on the branded skin, in case that made a difference, and spoke the strange-sounding words.

At first, I felt nothing.

Then, as loud and strong as the first time Vidar's thoughts entered my mind, they came again. *Rilla, my love. I do not know how to—but thank you. You may wish to sit down.*

Sit down? Why?

My head exploded with sensations. Wind whirled over my scales as it fought its way between the peaks.

Wait. What peaks? And since when did I have scales?

You don't. I do.

Only then did I realize that I could also still see the library and the map, like a ghost image on top of the mountainside. Unless I focused on the library, in which case, the mountainside became a ghost image atop the library.

I fumbled my way into the desk chair. "Will it always be like this?"

Nay, only when we do a working together. Focus on the wall, my Rilla.

On the wall. Of course. The whole reason I'd—well—married him. Not that it felt exactly like a marriage. Enough about that. I needed to focus. I concentrated on the map in the library.

No, my Rilla. On the real wall.

I looked at the mountainside through Vidar's eyes, but I could see nothing.

We must use our magic eyes to see the wall.

Our magic eyes? Did I even have magic eyes?

You're too agitated, dearest. Remember Lesson One.

Lesson One? He thought I should do that idiotic breathing exercise? Fine. I breathed in. Held it. Out. Held it.

You're doing very well. Now, stretch out with the eyes of your mind.

This was idiotic. Eyes didn't stretch. Fingers stretched.

With the fingers of your mind, then. Will yourself to see all that is there.

All that was there. Right. It was as if I were trying to lift a limb I didn't even have. I breathed slow and strained, and something flickered before me.

That's nearly it. Keep it up.

I slowed my breathing even farther and reached out with phantom fingers.

There.

Right across the mountain pass ahead of Vidar, and running up the peaks on either side, rose an infinitely tall wall of polished black stone, sprinkled with gems of other colors, mostly green.

Beautiful. Now join your magic to mine to strengthen the protection.

I had no more idea how to do that than I'd known how to see the wall.

Feel the magic within you, and let it flow outward, like a mountain stream.

I hadn't believed I had any magic until a few days ago, but I had sent the warning, hadn't I? There must have been something there. Though what my trifling magic could add to Vidar's, I didn't know.

Bound pairs are always stronger together than the simple sum of their power.

"If you say so."

I stared at the wall with my strange new vision and reached within myself with those fingers that had no substance until I felt something cool, almost liquid. That must have been my magic. I forced it outward, toward the wall, and soon I could see it as a thin trickle of gold that flowed out to join what?

Then I saw it, the thick beam of shiny black and green that sprang from Vidar's heart and disappeared into the wall.

I directed my own tiny flow toward his. When they met, it felt as if my entire body warmed. Vidar's beam grew, doubling and then tripling in size, and taking on strands of gold. My body felt light. So light indeed, that my feet lifted from the floor.

Unlike when I'd worked magic on my own, however, I did not lose energy, but rather gained it. My trickle of magic became a stream, and the joint flow grew to the size of an ancient tree trunk.

My perception of the wall intensified, and I could feel all along it, sense the improvements we had made, almost as if I now had three bodies pulsing with sensation all along them.

My own.

Vidar's.

And the wall.

The magic expanded and sped the thickening along the circuit in both directions, speeding the wall expansion toward a point opposite Vidar.

The sensations overwhelmed me, and I struggled to maintain my focus on the wall when these many sights and sounds and feelings flooded my mind. How long could I keep doing this?

We had to finish before Adramelech arrived. But I could spare no attention to check on his progress. I could barely focus on the job at hand. I prayed (here I was, praying again) that we would finish in time.

The first few minutes were the hardest. Once I'd learned the trick of directing my attention and joining my magic to Vidar's, it became easier. The odd sensation of multiple perspectives became less disorienting, and even our fortification of the wall went faster.

We rounded the last two corners and raced for the end point. We were within a few hundred miles. Then a hundred. Then fifty. Then ten. We were going to make it!

A shadow fell over the mountain, and pain laced through our back from our shoulder blades to our tail. We screamed, and the magical flow wavered.

"No!" I shouted, forcing my concentration away from the pain and into the magic.

The magic wavered, and our two streams began to separate.

I will not give up now! Vidar followed that thought with a string of incomprehensible words.

The stream of magic reunited more powerfully than ever.

Finish it, my Rilla. Vidar thought at me, and then the pain disappeared.

All of the power—his and mine—rushed from me, pouring into the wall, until the last gap closed, and a great golden net shot across the sky from the terminal point back to the start.

Only then did I realize that I could no longer feel Vidar. I felt myself. I felt the wall—all along the border. I held our power within myself.

But Vidar was nowhere.

Not even a thought from him tickled my mind.

CHAPTER TWENTY-FIVE

Library

anic rose in me. The river of power flowing from me stopped abruptly in a shower of black and gold sparks that danced through the library, tossing books off their shelves and turning off lights until the last of the crazy magic faded away. I stood in a darkened room, sensing nothing but the border wall which still occupied much of my mind. By practicing my breathing and focusing on the physical world around me, I returned my attention to the library, but a shadow of the wall remained in my mind. I was aware of an assault against it at Clear Eye Pass, but though the mountain shifted beneath the wall, the barrier held. I was glad, because even if the wall had fallen, I couldn't imagine anything more to do to shore it up. My time was better spent regaining my bearings and discovering what happened to Vidar. For that I would, at the very least, need light.

I stumbled toward a wall, doing I knew not what irreparable damage to the volumes I inadvertently stepped upon. Once I reached a wall, I followed it to the doorway. Pressing the usual spot on the wall did nothing to restore the lights, so I reached out with my magic, which had reverted to a tiny golden stream, though a larger one than I'd had at first. I wondered if some of Vidar's magic had transferred to me—or if magic grew with use.

It would be better to worry about the nature of magic another time. With the magic I still didn't understand, I willed the lights to repair themselves, not knowing if such a thing would have any effect or what it might cost me, but I had to try. How else would I see the map and the magic book that had to be returned to its bookcase before I could even leave this room?

For several long minutes, nothing happened.

Then a chime sounded, and the lights came up.

I almost wanted to turn them back off when I saw the disaster of ragged books the magic explosion had wrought. Taking a deep breath, I picked my way back through the mess to the map.

The boundary wall on the map stood thick and strong, exactly as it felt in my mind. Even at Clear Eye Pass, where I had been feeling assaults until a few minutes ago, the wall held. Instead of sitting atop a pass, though, the wall there rose up out of rubble, the remains of an avalanche. Every so often, on the Arkon side of the wall, a dragon form would emerge from the mountain and limp away, disappearing off the edge of the map. There was no sign of either Adramelech or Vidar. Like the dragons on the Arkon side, they must have been buried in the slide.

Over the next three hours, I watched thirty dragons emerge from the Arkon side and one purple dragon emerge on our side. Adramelech shrank to human size before disappearing from view. So, Adramelech still lived, though he'd returned to his human form. If I remembered correctly what Vidar had told me after their last fight, returning to human form meant Adramelech was severely injured and would take time to heal.

I reached for my magic to strengthen the protections I'd built against him in my mind. He was probably in no shape to come here for some time yet, but no doubt he would come eventually. I needed to be ready for him.

I had time, though. For now, I watched the map, picking up the tempest-tossed books whenever I couldn't bear to stare at the map any longer.

Some required repairs, but the same will that fixed the lights could restore torn pages and reattach spines. The chore—or perhaps the magic—exhausted me, though, and before I'd made much progress, I collapsed in the desk chair and fell asleep watching the map.

Vidar had still not appeared when I awoke, so I continued my cleaning and watching, breaking only to eat quick meals and change into fresh clothes now and then. When exhaustion set in, I'd sleep. Every time I awoke, I hoped to see Vidar emerging from under the mountain, but he never did.

I am not sure how many days I spent cleaning the library and watching the map, hoping against hope that Vidar would appear. I tried to connect with him in my mind, but no thoughts but my own sounded in my head.

The border wall buzzed in my mind, though, making me ever aware of the non-magical beings who passed through, and the magical ones who were held back. I could feel the barrier even in my sleep, humming against my consciousness, weaving through my dreams.

I wished I could remember more clearly what Vidar had said about me carrying the key to the wall. Was that what I was doing now? Certainly, I could still feel all along the wall, just as I had when we were strengthening it together. But I thought he'd said I would do this only if he was unable to. And what would make him unable to? Unconsciousness or death, wasn't it? Dared I dream he was unconscious? Or was he dead? Could even a dragon survive this long under the mountain?

Standing here worrying about it wouldn't help him and might make me insane, though. I finished picking up the last of the books, swept the floor, and turned my attention to the long-neglected kitchen. I started some bread to rise, straightened a few small messes around the house, and tried to decide what I should do next.

I would have liked to go up to the farm to tend the orchards, the greenhouse, and the sheep, but I wasn't at all sure I could get there without a dragon to fly me over the parts where Vidar had carried me. Besides, what would I do if Adramelech caught me out of Dragonhome? We hadn't had much time to strengthen the outer buildings.

The mountain above my head felt like it was pressing in on me, and I fought the feeling by staying busy baking, knitting, washing clothes, practicing magic, and strengthening the wall.

All the same, my spirits flagged, and every morning, if it could be called morning in a place where the sun never rose, it felt harder to rise from the giant bed on the floor, get dressed, and face the day.

Every morning, after clearing away my breakfast dishes, I went to the library and wrote with the magic feather on the map.

"Vidar, are you all right? Can I help you in any way?"

Every morning, the map stayed stubbornly blank.

CHAPTER TWENTY-SIX
Unwelcome Visitor

On the forty-fifth day since I'd started counting, I was still standing there, staring at the blank map, waiting for a response that was almost certain not to come, when Adramelech came to the farm.

He arrived in human form, as if appearing out of the mist, but then switched to dragon. I screamed in shock and anger as he crushed the greenhouse again.

"Stop that, you horrible brute," I shouted.

Certainly, if you're willing to talk with me.

Adramelech's thoughts felt slimy and intrusive in a way Vidar's never did. I obviously hadn't strengthened my mental defenses as much as I should.

You care for the weakling who abandoned you? How amusing.

"I don't have to talk to you," I muttered as I concentrated on thickening the walls in my mind.

I will eat all these tempting little sheep if you close yourself off from me again.

I sucked in a shaky breath. Why was I listening to this monster?

Because you get attached to things. If you don't want to see them hurt, you will treat with me.

"I won't."

A vision pressed in on me—more than a vision. Like when I had joined with Vidar, I felt scales and claws and a tail.

"I never agreed to join with you!" I tried to pull back from the vision, but it would not retreat from me, and I was forced to participate as my—no, his—right front claw swept across Little Lady's back, and she bleated in terror and pain.

Any dragon with fully formed powers can force a bond, you witless woman. I do not need your permission.

"I am Vidar's wife, not your slave!"

Are you sure of that?

To my dismay, a pain burned all around the base of my neck. I ran out of the library into the bedroom, so I could look in the mirror.

A marking circled my neck, more like a lacy collar than a necklace.

"No!" I scrubbed at it, but that only increased the burning.

In my head, Adramelech laughed.

"I refuse! I will never be yours!"

You are mine already.

I willed my mental walls against Adramelech to thicken, and his presence in my mind flickered. Before he disappeared completely, I felt him plunge his claw completely through Little Lady's heart.

"No!" I crumpled to the floor, sobbing.

A pain, like the one on my neck, burned across my left forearm. I turned it, and saw words, like the ones Vidar had written on the map, but darker and harsher. "Open back up to me, or I'll kill the others."

I couldn't. Even to save the sheep, I couldn't let Adramelech into my mind. Not now that I guarded the border. Much more than a few sheep would die if I let him and his like overrun our kingdom.

The writing on my arm disappeared, leaving a blurry red echo of itself, and fresh words seared my arm. "He's never returning. If he's not dead yet, he will be soon."

I turned my arm, so I couldn't see the message, but I couldn't stop thinking about it. The words put my fear into plain language. I'd long worried that Vidar had died under Clear Eye, and I would spend the rest of my days here, never seeing the sun or stars, never touching a tree or animal.

New pain ran across my arm, and though I resisted the urge to look at it for a while, eventually curiosity won out.

"You'll need my help to get out of that cave."

Did he still have access to my mind? How did he know how trapped I felt down here?

Though truly, if I wanted to leave, I could. The library held maps that showed the way to the surface. I had chosen not to go up. The only reason I hadn't left was that I wasn't sure I could protect myself and the wall from Adramelech up there.

A giant rumbling filled the air around me. The mountain itself roared and vibrated. I covered my ears and crouched before the mirror, fully expecting the mountain to fall on my head, trapping me in this hole beneath the earth.

This went on for minutes—hours—I don't know. Intolerably long.

Then, the rumbling died down.

Dragonhome remained intact, and I straightened out, relieved that I had survived, not realizing in my initial relief that the mountain had indeed fallen on my head, trapping me in this hole beneath the earth.

CHAPTER TWENTY-SEVEN

Research

t took me a bit to fully realize the extent of my losses. The first sign was a burning pain that streaked across my forearm just as I was beginning to hope I'd escaped whatever doom Adramelech had planned for me. I lifted my arm, and there, in dark black scrawled on the inflamed remains of previous messages, Adramelech had seared, "Call me when you're ready to come out."

I would never be ready to come out if it meant submitting to Adramelech. I returned to the library to see if there was anything I could do to remove his messages and markings from my body and his foul magic from my mind.

There, of course, in front of the magic books, was our map, and on it, the farm had been reduced to a pile of rubble. I could see no barns, no greenhouse, no orchards, and no sheep. Indeed, the basin itself seemed to have collapsed inward, the mountains all around it crumbled, their pulverized peaks filling in the fertile land. I saw nothing moving except Adramelech, retreating from the wreckage as if his job here was done.

"Stay away!" I said, and for once, I hoped he could hear me.

No, I didn't.

I just wanted him gone.

At that moment, I felt an assault on the border wall from the Arkon side, and I was almost glad of it—of having something to do other than catalog what I'd lost in this latest attack.

With a bit of infused magic, the wall stood firm, and soon I was left to myself and the books and the map.

I could not find a single one of the sheep Vidar had caught for me, nor any of their babies. As I wept, I found myself hoping that their ends had been quick.

When my tears ran dry, I went to see how the cavern outside the human side of Dragonhome had fared. The door opened to my touch, but only halfway, and beyond it sat what looked like a solid mound of rocks. It started to shift, and I quickly closed the door. On the other side, rocks rolled and rumbled and then were still.

I was certainly not getting out of here on my own. Only a dragon could reach me.

I crept backward into Dragonhome, trembling. I refused to think about what this all meant. Not yet. Exhausted more by overwhelming emotions than by exertion, I sought out the nest and slept.

I awoke in the dark, my heart racing, sure that I was being buried alive, but when I found the room lights, all was as I had left it. I calmed, but only until I remembered that I was indeed buried alive—just with all of Dragonhome intact. Adramelech had imprisoned me here by bringing the mountain down atop me.

A panic rose in me, but I tamped it back down. Remaining here would drive me mad, but there was no way out without accepting help from Adramelech.

Or was there?

I hurried through my morning ablutions and rushed to the library. I saw no sign of Vidar, and I had little hope as I wrote my daily message to him. I wrote my usual note, but then I added an account of what Adramelech had done to Dragonhome and to me. I assured Vidar that I would find a way to wipe Adramelech's marks from my skin. I would cut off his access to my arm.

Even if it killed me, I would erase Adramelech's influence in my life.

The background hum of the border wall swelled to a throbbing in my mind. What would happen to it if I died?

I supposed I'd better find out before I did anything that might end up in my death. I did not mind dying if it would rid me of a monster, but I would mind it if my death empowered that monster to break down the wall.

So, my goals were securing the border and cleansing myself of these unwanted bonds. I needed to know how to do both. Surely, something in this magical library could tell me.

I threw myself into the research, reading all day and all night, for untold days, barely sleeping, and eating but little. My eyes grew red, and my temper short, but there wasn't much to vent the latter on except the books, and I needed them too much to do any real damage.

In a restless, angry mood after hours of fruitless research, I explored the house again, and came upon a giant gymnasium I had not seen before. It had a sheer rock in the center whose purpose I could not guess, but off to one side hung a column-shaped bag full of sand, like the ones castle guards would sometimes pummel during their training sessions.

Perfect.

I punched and kicked at the thing until my knuckles were raw, and my breath came in gasps. I needed rest. I would think better after sleeping anyway.

In the morning, anger still filled me, but my mind felt clear, and I'd thought up a way to quickly survey the magical books for what I needed. Then I could carefully read only the most likely to be useful.

Even with the new system, it was slow going, especially as I stopped now and then to take regular meals, beat at the poor punching column, and sleep. I sent daily reports to Vidar as well, and though he never responded, I felt close to him. His mark on my collarbone seemed to be growing, and where it touched Adramelech's collar, the hated marks faded away.

I found this hopeful and told myself it was a sign that Vidar wasn't dead, though what did I know of such things? Still, hope refused to die, even when, one afternoon while I was kicking the stuffing out of the punching column, words burned across my forearm again.

CHAPTER TWENTY-EIGHT

Hoping

"Ready to see the stars again?" The words burned across my forearm.

Evil dragon. I would never see stars again if the price of doing so was submitting to him. Surely, Adramelech realized that by now?

He must have been hoping I'd change my mind, for after that point, the messages came several times a day.

"I could rescue you from that mausoleum."

"Let me come for you. I will make you a garden."

"Even the strongest of dragon retreats can collapse under the weight of a mountain if no dragon tends it."

That threat frightened me. Not so much that I answered Adramelech, but enough that I began looking for information on tending to dragon retreats in addition to searching for ways to reverse dragon bonds.

At least this new search was easy. Within an hour, I had books and books on everything from safely reforming rocks and digging tunnels to building artificial caverns and keeping support structures strong. Many of these tasks had notations in the margins in Vidar's father's crabbed hand, and I soon realized that in addition to providing helpful notes, he'd also marked each set of instructions with a number to show which level in *First Steps*, *Intermediate Steps*, or *Advanced Steps* a magic user needed to reach before attempting the work. Apparently, Vidar's father didn't want his offspring endangering themselves by trying to use magic beyond their grasp.

I assumed, perhaps arrogantly, that the notations would apply to me as well as to young dragons and was glad to see that some of the maintenance magic was already within my ability. For others, I needed to progress only a few chapters more. I added magic lessons and work on Dragonhome into my routine. Days went by in study, research, punching out my frustrations, tending to personal needs, and trying to ignore Adramelech's writing on my arm.

"Are you finding things to do down there?"

I laughed aloud at that one for a long moment. Adramelech really must not have access to my mind any longer, which I supposed accounted for the searing words on my forearm. Well, he could just keep wondering what I was thinking. I was busy. I returned my attention to the maintenance web I'd been focused on building. I had passed the magic lessons needed for it only that morning, and I was eager to try it.

I started by calming myself with prayer. I didn't remember when I'd begun to do that. Perhaps it was the time alone that had me taking up the religious habits of my parents, just as it had me writing long screeds to Vidar on the map each morning.

But the prayer before magic seemed like more than a call out into the darkness in hope of touching someone other than Adramelech. It was also a cry for direction—a request that as I played with powers greater than I had ever imagined touching, that those powers change me and the world around me only in good and healthy ways.

It was true that I feared being crushed by tons of stone. I feared living alone, unremembered and entombed miles beneath the earth, for the rest of my days. I feared being enslaved and abused by Adramelech.

But more than all that, I feared becoming as much of a monster as he was.

And if there was one thing I had learned about magic use, it was that it couldn't be done in fear. So, I prayed. I told my Creator my fears and my hopes. I asked him for strength, for resolve, for insight. And I asked that my endeavors—the work of my hands and my magic, the words of my mouth, and the very thoughts in my heart would please him.

Only then was I free enough of the fear that I could do my breathing, find my magic, and direct it to the task at hand.

I expected the maintenance web to be tricky, but it came easily, naturally. I soon realized why. It was the same as the first big magic I'd ever done—seeing and growing the wall that Vidar was working on. Soon the shadow of the border wall that lived in my mind was joined by the shadow of Dragonhome, both the human side and the collapsed cavern that had led to the human dwelling.

Unlike the shadow wall, this shadow home refused to fade into the background. The outer cavern screamed its distress at me. I wondered if this pain would lessen as I got used to it or if the pain would only fade if I repaired the entrance cave.

I hoped it was the former, for fixing the cavern was far beyond my skill.

CHAPTER TWENTY-NINE

Messages

ou will run out of food sometime."

Well, wasn't that a cheerful thought? Though as it happened, it wasn't true. I rubbed the searing words even though I knew from painful experience that this would only make them hurt more in the long run. I had yet to find a salve or cream—or a recipe for one— that would ease the sting of Adramelech's cursed words. The literal sting, that is.

Besides the physical pain, these words had no power over me. Several days earlier, I had worried about this on my own and gone looking for magic to ease the problem. I'd found instructions for enchanting containers of food or drink so that they would replace whatever was used. The magic itself was beyond me—for the moment— but once I'd seen the instructions, I realized that all the grain, several of the jugs of milk and juice, many of the cheeses, and most of the dried fruits and vegetables were already stored in this kind of container. I could eat, and eat well, until the end of my days.

What I couldn't do was fix the entrance cave to Dragonhome. At least not yet. The persistent chafing of the rubble on my mind spurred me to devise a plan for repair, and I thought I had found all the instructions I would need—enchantments for stabilizing structures, for pulverizing or relocating earth, for creating systems of caves and tunnels, for strengthening the surrounding mountain, and for regrowing cave formations. I was very glad to find that last thing. Apart from safety, the only thing I had appreciated about the dragon side of Dragonhome was the amazing pearly structures that were now buried in rubble. It warmed me to know that I might be able to regrow them.

Unfortunately, every part of that magic was too difficult for me, though I might be able to stabilize what was already here with another week or two of practice. I certainly would if my progress continued at its current rate.

As I practiced that morning, I noticed that my stream of magic appeared thicker. Not nearly as thick as Vidar's had been, but much heftier than my original little gold trickle. Maybe magic was like muscle—it grew stronger with use.

I wished my searches for a way to remove Adramelech's slave mark and block his access to my arm were as productive as my magical education and plans to restore Dragonhome. Unfortunately, afternoon after afternoon of scanning books yielded nothing useful.

Well, nothing to the point. I learned many useful things—how to create and repair the running water, for example. I also learned many spells for growing things and bringing rain. Equally useful when Adramelech was near were the magic shields and weapons I found. I wasn't sure how much use they'd be if Adramelech ever found his way to me, but they would be better than facing him with nothing.

How I wished we had known this magic before our farm was attacked. Didn't Vidar's father realize how important it was for people to be able to defend themselves against the likes of Adramelech?

Perhaps the old dragon thought his border wall was protection enough. Or perhaps he feared people armed with magic that could destroy dragons. Certainly, if my father and brothers had known such magic, they would have used it on any dragon that came within sight, no matter who that dragon was. My family would have considered Vidar just as much their enemy as Adramelech.

At least until they got to know him.

But they wouldn't have gotten to know him.

However, if dragons and other people lived alongside each other instead of firmly apart, my family would have had the chance to meet Vidar or other decent dragons. They would have realized that not all dragons were the same, just as not all people were the same.

I wrote an extra letter to Vidar that night, letting my thoughts spill into invisible map words. When I'd wrung all my anger and worry out, I stood there a while, leaning my head against the map. "Vidar, please come back to me," I whispered.

"He's dead, you know. There is no one but me to come for you."

Had Adramelech heard me somehow, or had he just made a very good guess about how I might be feeling?

Either way, the words burned into my skin, hurting more than any of the ones before because underneath my hope, this was the fear that gnawed at me. Being alone now, tomorrow, and forever.

Even that didn't hurt as much as the thought that Vidar might be dead.

I didn't want to lose him.

You will not.

"Vidar! Vidar!"

There was no answer. Had I imagined him? The thoughts had sounded far away and quiet, but I'd heard them clearly. I was sure. At least I thought I was.

"He's gone."

These words came so soon after Adramelech's previous ones that beneath them, my arm glowed angry red.

It wasn't true.

I refused to believe it.

Even if it was true, I was going to act as if it were not, as if Vidar could read my letters, as if I had heard his voice.

As if he were coming home.

CHAPTER THIRTY

Craziness

prayed I wasn't going insane.

I'd heard him, hadn't I? I'd been so sure at first, but as days went by, and I heard nothing else, that moment of connection felt less and less real.

And yet, every morning and evening, as I wrote my message to Vidar, his mark grew, the sunny rays spreading out from the original mark. Adramelech's collar receded until nothing was left of it but an inch-wide band of purple that circled my neck. Soon that would be gone as well, I hoped.

I held onto this belief, repeating it to myself as evidence that Vidar was still out there, somewhere. How could he not be when I could see the proof of our connection growing in my very skin?

Vidar's expanding mark wasn't the only change in my skin. A network of glowing gold lines crisscrossed every part of me that I could see, even my face. It wasn't obvious when I looked directly in the mirror, but when I viewed myself at a slant, I could see the glow of gold just beneath my skin. Every time I practiced magic, the lines grew thicker, and new ones formed. Before long, my skin would be mostly gold.

Though this alteration disconcerted me, the changes wouldn't stop me from working magic now that I'd learned what it would take to stabilize the cavern. I spent long hours pulverizing boulders and blowing the fragments off to nearby cracks, crevices, and caves.

It was exhausting work that strained my magic and hardly seemed to make a difference. With my shadow-senses, I could feel a tiny opening at the top of Dragonhome's outer cavern, but though I worked steadily at it, the cleared space seemed to stay the same size. I could calculate mathematically that I was removing more and more—doubling how much I cleared away with every passing day. But after working harder than a plow ox for a week, there was no discernible difference in the rubble blocking the cave. Nor was I finding anything about dragon marks in my research. My sleep was restless, my food had no flavor, and Adramelech's painful and depressing notes interrupted me several times a day.

At the end of the second week, the tiny hole at the top of the cavern seemed no bigger, though I knew it had grown. My measurements suggested I'd cleared sixty farmhouses of space, but compared to what remained, that felt like nothing.

Not all was bad, though. The golden network of lines just beneath my skin was starting to cut through Adramelech's messages, and where the lines passed, the skin wouldn't burn. Even if I never opened up the cavern, this was reason enough to keep at my work. Plus, once or twice, I thought I heard Vidar's voice in my mind again. The first time, I thought I heard, *Thank you, my Rilla,* and the second time, it was, *You are so amazing.*

I didn't feel amazing. Especially when my rubble clearing seemed to have profited me only a smidgeon more of open space. Oh, my math equations told me that the tiny hole at the top of the cavern could now hold all the homes and barns from my village—and then some, but it didn't feel that way.

Don't give up. You are closer than you realize.

Lovely. Now, I was not only imagining Vidar in my mind, but I was imagining him saying crazy things. I wrote this in my note to him that night and thought I heard him chuckle.

That, at least, was the kind of thing he'd actually do.

My arm itched, and I looked down. Adramelech's words were so blocked by golden lines, that I could barely make them out.

"It is a mistake to live and die completely alone. It will drive you insane."

"Then insane I will have to be," I said aloud.

Then I sighed.

It was lonely down here.

CHAPTER THIRTY-ONE

Threats

My third week of excavation started out no more productive than the first two, but by day four, I thought I could see a significant chunk of the rock missing. On the fifth day of that third week, I made as much headway as in all the days before. Then on the sixth day, my work saw the cavern nearly halfway empty. By the end of the seventh day, I was so close to finishing that I kept going instead of returning inside and researching how to remove dragon marks.

Shortly after my usual time for dinner, the cavern was clear. I opened the door and stepped out into the space. Darkness swallowed my candlelight, but I could sense the vastness. Vidar could fly here, though it wouldn't be as pretty as before. No columns jutted up from the floor or speared downward from the ceiling, and not even a glimmer remained of the pearly sheen that had once adorned the place.

That was a problem for another day. I sat there in the huge empty space, exhausted, but proud of what I had done.

And hopeful.

After all, if I had cleared the cave, I could travel to the surface.

Where Adramelech waited to gobble me up. Though, that wasn't likely, seeing how he could have eaten me at our first encounter. He must have had a much more sinister purpose in mind for me.

I shivered.

Whatever it was, I wanted no part of it. I wouldn't move from my refuge until I'd learned how to solve my dragon problem.

Retreating into the human side of Dragonhome, I prepared a simple meal, washed up, exercised in the gym, read some from one of the library's histories and from the Good Book, and settled in for the night.

The next day, I still felt exhausted, and I could sense no immediately pressing issues with either the border wall or Dragonhome, so I took the day off. I napped and dyed some white wool green to match the color of Vidar's eyes.

It was silly to make a sweater for a dragon who might be dead, and who couldn't change to his human form even if he wasn't.

My arm itched, and I scratched it. Hours later, I noticed the barely legible words, "Your friends miss you."

My friends? Those girls from the castle? I wasn't sure I'd call them friends. Especially not Alvina, who had always seemed more like a jealous rival than a friend. All the same, I hoped they were well. Even Alvina didn't deserve to be the victim of Sir Drake's depredations.

My arm itched again. Since I was looking at it already, I saw the words scroll across. "You remember Alvina, Bria, and Kali, don't you? Poor, deluded young ladies. Their families have sold them to me, but I grow tired of them as I would never grow tired of you, my sweet."

I scowled. I wasn't his sweet, and I had no desire to be his sweet. And what would he do with the girls if he was getting tired of them? Why bother to tell me about it?

The words on my arm blurred out once more, and another set started. Between the redness and the gold strands in my skin, it was hard to make the new words out, but I pieced the letters together until I read, "I shall begin my games in one week unless you return and need my castoffs to serve, once again, as your ladies' maids."

Evil, evil beast.

My heart cried out for the girls, especially Bria, who had never been anything but kind to me. But how could I give myself up to Adramelech? There was more at stake than the girls' lives and my own. If Adramelech gained power over the border wall and Dragonhome through me, my country, Heshal, could become as evil a place as Arkon.

I could not allow that to happen.

But I couldn't allow Adramelech to torture the palace girls, either.

I had a week to end him, and I hadn't the faintest idea how it could be accomplished.

Never before had a week felt like such little time.

CHAPTER THIRTY-TWO

Kill the Dragon

he library was full to the brim with ideas of how to kill dragons—usually couched in warnings about what a young dragon should beware of.

Unfortunately, most of these ideas could only be implemented by another dragon. I could not plunge my claw into a dragon's heart or rip off an opponent's wings when the two of us were halfway to the moon. Injecting poison into an opponent's eye seemed more promising. I could paint an arrow with a sufficiently deadly poison and possibly get a shot off before Adramelech could kill me. The only poisons sufficiently deadly, however, were venom from green and orange dragons, and Dragonhome didn't contain any. I had checked every version of Dragonhome's inventory. I supposed that since Vidar and his family were black dragons, and they hadn't been in dragon society for some time before Adramelech's first attack against their farm, they would have had few opportunities to obtain such poisons.

And perhaps Vidar's father hadn't been comfortable with having such dangerous substances lying around. He seemed the overprotective sort, leaving dozens upon dozens of rules that all started with "never."

Never blow fire in or at a human habitation.

Never shift in a building that is too small to hold you.

Never love a woman for her physical beauty alone.

Never fly higher than the air.

Never pick a fight with an older or a stronger dragon.

Never fail to aid a family member who needs assistance.

Never allow a woman to progress beyond *First Steps* in magic.

Wait—what?

I was already halfway through *Intermediate Steps*. Was this a danger to dragons, or to myself, or to both?

Hoping the danger would be to dragons, I quickly scanned books until I found four that dealt with women and magic.

There I found my answers. When a woman's magic became strong, that magic would erode any bonds between herself and a dragon. If she performed magic strong enough, she could break a bond outright, and that would kill the dragon she was bonded with.

The purple line that circled my neck was proof that Adramelech had bonded with me. If I performed strong enough magic in a single moment, I could erase that line completely, killing the evil old beast in the process.

Of course, any magic big enough to break the bond with Adramelech would also break the bond with Vidar.

Killing him, too.

CHAPTER THIRTY-THREE
Big Magic

*idar is already dead*, a part of me whispered, but I didn't believe it. Not completely. Perhaps I'd imagined his thoughts. Perhaps, the strengthening of his mark when I wrote to him meant nothing.

Or perhaps, he was still out there, and my magic use had been weakening him, keeping him from coming home to me.

I didn't want to sacrifice Vidar to save the palace girls. They weren't half as much my friends as he was. But could I live with sacrificing them to save him? Especially if such an action might not even save him? He might already be dead.

I kept looking for other ways to kill Adramelech. I also read everything I could that touched on women, magic, and bonding marks.

I found dozens more ways to kill Adramelech, but most depended on dragon strength or skill. The few others I located required great bursts of magic that were probably beyond my ability and that were certainly past the threshold of what would be safe for Vidar.

Late that night, I found a notation in Vidar's father's journal that mentioned, in passing, a friend who had married a sorceress. Apparently, the woman had marked the friend with the same bonding spell that dragons used to mark wives. A husband spell.

If I remade a bond with Vidar at the same time I broke one, would that keep our connection strong enough that he would not die? I was not sure, and I didn't like risking him, but I looked for instructions on how dragons made wife bonds anyway. If I couldn't find something better, this might be worth trying. Possibly risking Vidar was better than certainly killing him.

I found the instructions for wife-bond magic easily, but once I located them, my dilemma increased. The magic required was *Advanced Steps*, Lesson Twelve. I had half the intermediate book yet to finish. Certainly, the magic would be strong enough to break my current bonds, but I wasn't sure I could do it. I couldn't practice other magic to work up to it, either, for I didn't know how doing that magic might affect Vidar.

I also wondered how much I really wanted to strengthen my bond with Vidar.

I liked Vidar, and I wanted to do what was best for him, but committing to someone for life was hard.

Risky as it was for Vidar and for me, I would do it if no other viable options presented themselves. For now, though, I returned to my books to see if I could find anything that would kill Adramelech while not using more magic than I had already mastered. Vidar seemed to have survived this far well enough. At least I thought he had. Hoped he had.

Over the next two days, I found several dozen more ideas of how a dragon could be killed, but none of them suited my purpose. Most of them required the one doing the killing to be a dragon himself. A few required highly advanced magic. Several required a dragon to perform advanced magic.

I had just picked up a new book to scan when itchy words slid across my skin.

"I am tired of waiting. Ask me to rescue you now, or I will begin with Alvina."

He'd said I had a week!

Why did it surprise me that he would lie?

Maybe he was lying about beginning to torture Alvina, too. But could I take that chance?

I hadn't yet found any way to kill Adramelech without also killing Vidar except to perform a husband bond on Vidar.

There was no guarantee it would work, seeing how Vidar wasn't here, and I'd have to reach him through the mark he'd put on me. Even if it did work, it might not be enough magic to kill Adramelech. I doubted Adramelech was as attached to me as Vidar, even if he had marked me.

And that was assuming I was able to perform the magic. Perhaps, instead, I would kill myself trying to perform the enchantment, and not manage to forge a new link with Vidar after all.

But any magic strong enough to kill me would break my bond with Adramelech, which meant that even in the event that he survived me, he would not be able to use the bond to gain access to this library or the border wall. And it would hurt him. Enough, probably, to stop his torture of Alvina.

I hoped the girls would use the reprieve to escape.

I prayed to focus and rid myself of fear, did my breathing exercises, and then directed my magic at the dragon mark Vidar had given me. I worried that I would not know how to weave the web of connection the enchantment called for. I touched Vidar's mark, and realized that a bond to him lived there. I needed only to strengthen and expand it. I directed my magic at myself, sending golden magic along each ebony path, and whispering words of commitment to Vidar as if he could hear me. "I will love you. I will support you. I will build a future with you. We will walk this road of life together, sharing in all things—joys and sorrows, plenty and want, sickness and health—from now until the Creator takes one of us home."

Vidar's dragon mark burned hot in my skin, flowing up my neck and down my chest, obliterating the collar-like mark Adramelech had placed there, but butting hard against something deeper, like a stone set next to my heart—a purple stone. When my magic reached it, the stream thinned and though the stone began to dissolve, it would not be enough. "Vidar, help me," I whispered.

Always, my love.

Magic, dark as thunder clouds that bring rain swelled my gold stream, and in moments, the stone I felt within me dissolved like a lump of sand in a flood. The bonding spell washed upward through my head and downward over the rest of me, until my whole body glowed with hot golden light so intense, I could hardly bear it. This light, I shot toward Vidar, who I could now feel emerging from the collapsed mountain where Clear Eye Pass had been. His wings were twisted and ragged, and his scales broken and dull, but he wore no collar, and when my bond reached him, the gold light sank into him, and he staggered, while the bond I sent, powered by both our magic, edged all his scales with gold.

And it was done.

You've given me a dragon mark, Vidar thought at me as the magic, finished with its work, ricocheted about the library as uncontrollably as the time I'd stopped working on the wall.

Books rained all around me, and the lights brightened, and then exploded, leaving me in darkness.

Not again.

I collapsed on the floor, hoping that I'd been as successful at killing Adramelech as I'd been at forging the bond with Vidar.

Successful.

I'd been successful, but Vidar hadn't sounded entirely pleased.

Why wouldn't he be?

The thought troubled me as I drifted off into unconsciousness.

CHAPTER THIRTY-FOUR
Wife Bonds

 *illa! Rilla!*

"Vidar? Are you here?" I wasn't even sure where *here* was. I lay in darkness on a lumpy, uncomfortable surface.

Thank the Creator. I thought you died.

No. I didn't think I was dead. Surely dead people would have fewer aches in their back, and head, and legs, and—well, everywhere. Still, if I hurt, I was alive. "So, you're all right, and I'm all right. Did I manage to kill Adramelech?"

Very nearly. He was so weak when I found him that it was a simple matter to finish him. I didn't even need to take dragon form. Though he did. The palace was in quite an uproar about it when I left.

"Did Alvina, Bria, and Kali survive?"

Alvina, Bria, and Kali?

"The girls Adramelech was threatening to torture if I did not ask him to come rescue me. I knew that if I gave him access to me and to Dragonhome, he'd gain control of your father's library and the wall, and I couldn't let that happen. But I also had to keep him from hurting the girls. They're not good friends, but I know them." I pictured the palace girls in their frilly dresses, hoping Vidar would catch the image.

Oh, Adramelech's pets. They were chained up in his quarters without food or water when I sought out our enemy. The young ladies all showed signs of recent abuse, but they assured me that only their confinement was out of the ordinary.

I remembered what Bria had told me about Sir Drake punishing her and gagged. "Did you set them free?"

I did not think it wise. They were all well under Adramelech's control and would likely have turned against me.

"But you've killed him now, right? They can be safely set free."

The mob that is tearing apart his rooms will no doubt find them soon. It will go better for the young ladies if the crowd can see that they were Sir Drake's victims, not his accomplices.

"The mob won't hurt them?"

Not if it finds them bound and battered, as it will.

I sucked in a deep breath. "Are you sure?"

I felt a wave of annoyance from Vidar. *This is clearly important to you, and you have made it so that I cannot ignore what is important to you.*

"Why would you want to ignore what is important to me?"

It is foolish to care for women who are most likely still loyal to a monster.

"Adramelech's enchantments hold after his death?"

Possibly.

"But that's not their fault! Don't you think they've been through enough already?"

It is not my business.

Infuriating dragon. And I didn't know of any way I could help the girls from here. I could tunnel my way out, of course, but that would require me finding enough energy to get off this floor and do the magic. That would take weeks, and it would be weeks more getting to the palace. I wouldn't be able to do any more than find out what had become of them and offer what assistance I could if any had escaped. It wasn't enough, but at least I could do that.

You could use my presence and my magic to help them.

"You just said it wasn't your business. You don't want to help."

You successfully completed a bond with me. My magic is at your disposal just as much as yours is at mine.

"What? I thought you were able to use my magic because I offered it."

I was able to use your magic because the wife bond existed. You agreed to the wife bond. I never agreed to any such thing.

"You asked me to surrender my magic to you WITHOUT you doing the same for me?!" I yelled, standing up and fumbling around in the dark, trying to find the library entrance.

Dragons do not willingly become puppets!

"Neither do human women! Were you trying to make me a puppet when you gave me a wife mark?" Adramelech was surely meaning to make me his puppet when he marked me, but was that Vidar's intention as well?

That wasn't the reason I marked you! You were sick, and it was the only way I knew of to heal you! Vidar thought at me. However, I could feel a wall falling as Vidar blocked me from the remainder of his thoughts. The barrier radiated pain through every part of me, but none of that agony felt as intense as the torment of what he tried to hide from me—that though he'd marked me because he wanted to heal me and remain my companion, he had, in fact, knowingly made me his puppet. And then had the audacity to be offended when I returned the favor! The pain in my core and limbs tightened its grip on me as Vidar's wall thickened.

So, this was what it felt like when one forged a bond with someone, and they cut one off. I understood what Vidar meant about actually dying from being separated from me. For surely, I would die from being separated from him. Perhaps I should have used another enchantment to remove Adramelech's bond with me—one that would have broken Vidar's as well.

No, I couldn't have borne being the cause of his death, or even his pain.

My suffering increased, and I laughed hollowly to myself. It was a pity Vidar didn't seem to mind killing me as much as I minded killing him.

Ah, well, I had long since come to terms with Dragonhome being my tomb.

Too bad I'd never see the stars again.

CHAPTER THIRTY-FIVE

Reconciliation

My eyes opened upon blackness, and for a moment, I thought I remained in the library, but softness pillowed me, and my aches had gone. Heaven?

"Hardly. You're still in Dragonhome." The voice was Vidar's, but it came to my ears, not my mind.

He chuckled, and light grew all around me, illuminating the silky green nest and a tall man with dark hair and eyes I recognized. "Vidar?" I sat up.

He dropped beside me and pulled me into his arms. "I was so worried. You've been asleep for weeks. I'm so sorry."

"For blocking me out of your mind until I nearly died?"

"Of course. And for not explaining about the marks well enough that you knew what you were agreeing to when I asked you to accept them. And for asking you for a commitment I wasn't willing to take on myself."

"I don't want to make you a puppet. I want us to work together. That's what I thought the mark meant," I said.

"That's what it will mean, for us. I never want you to feel again that it would have been better to have broken my bond with you when you broke Adramelech's."

"I only felt that way for an instant."

"It was a devastating instant." Vidar leaned in and kissed me.

After a moment, I kissed back.

When we came up for air, he said, "I made myself invisible, returned to the castle, and watched over your friends. When the mob found them, it released the women and saw them tended to and fed. They seemed in good hands when I left, but if you like, we can look in on them in a few weeks to make sure they are still doing well."

"Are you sure?"

"Positive."

I yanked him toward me for another kiss.

This one lasted longer than the first, and when it was finished, I lay back in the nest, unexpectedly worn out.

"I forgot you are still recovering." Vidar smiled. "Let's get some food into you, so that you're well enough for a trip outside."

I struggled to sit up. Walking was not going to be easy.

"Don't worry. I'll carry you. It's high time you saw stars again.

Epilogue
Summer of the following year

t took nearly a year to put the farm to rights after Adramelech's fall, even with our combined magic. But, on a cool evening in late summer, after a long day of harvesting dragonwheat, Vidar and I sat on a knoll overlooking the farm and declared the restoration complete. Golden sunlight glinted off the greenhouse windows, and a new flock of sheep grazed the hill below us. The orchard sprouted toward the skies as if it meant to make one year make do for twenty, and the mountains had resumed their previous shape. But, perhaps best of all, heavily laden vines covered the grape arbor, and tomorrow we would be making raisins.

"I wish our families could see this," I said.

"Me too," Vidar answered.

"Even with them gone, it feels so perfect."

"Nearly," he said.

"What else is missing?"

"Children." He nuzzled my neck.

"We could do something about that," I said.

"Are you sure? You know bearing wyrmlings takes longer and is more difficult than having ordinary human babies."

"I know." How could I not? Vidar had insisted I read every word in the library on the subject, and he had told me all he could remember of what his mother had told him. He didn't want me to make another commitment without knowing what I was agreeing to. I smiled up at him. "I know it will be long, and hard, but it will be worth it."

And it was.

✧   ✧

If you liked *Dragonpets: The Sacrifice,*
it would be super helpful if you could
leave a review. Thanks so much!

Acknowledgments
Seriously, Thank you

As solitary as writing can sometimes feel, the production of a book is never something I can accomplish entirely on my own. So here are a few of the many people who made this book possible.

First of all, God, who makes and inspires all good things.

Second, my sweet love, Craig, and my kids, who have been wonderfully understanding when I'm holed up with a book instead of doing things around the house that I probably should.

Third, for beta readers and critique partners--Isaac, Jill, David & Judith—who have provided insightful comments and great encouragement.

Fourth, Andrea Leeth, my wonderful copyeditor.

Fifth, you my readers, who make this a much less lonely pursuit than it would otherwise be.

And finally, I want to give a special shout out to Katie, who has been one of my most joyful, encouraging, interested readers.

You all make both my writing and my life better.

About the Author

R. L. S. Hoff

R. L. S. Hoff writes young adult science fiction and fantasy with strange worlds, stranger creatures, bits of romance…

…and princesses, of course.

She lives in a multi-cultural household where she sometimes has to remind one child that he must learn English because it's important for life in the US—and the other children that they must learn Mandarin because it is and always will be their brother's native language.

R. L. S. Hoff and her family live in a just-big-enough house with a messy yard in view of the Rocky Mountains. They keep planning to hike in the hills on weekends but often get no farther than the park across the street.

When not writing or working at (so far) more profitable gigs, R. L. S. Hoff enjoys reading, gardening, and baking bread.

pencilprincessworkshop.com

Other Books by R.L.S. Hoff

The Dicrandia Chronicles

Songs of Healing

The Golden Terrace Colony Series

Leaving Hope

StarRacer

SNEAK PEEK!

SONGS OF INNOCENCE

by RLS Hoff

CHAPTER ONE

Straltia

Something flickered at the edges of my vision. For the first time in the months I'd been doing Sarah Tressarian's hair, I dropped the brush. Sarah's whole updo came crashing down.

"Is everything all right, Straltia?" Sarah asked.

"Probably," I said. I faced the mirror where I thought I'd seen movement. Nothing there. Just my own reflection and the reflection of the youngest monarch in Dicrandia's short history.

I shook my head. "You do have protective walls around this room, don't you, Your Majesty?"

"Of course," Sarah said.

I retrieved the silver-backed brush and hoped it wasn't obvious how much I was trembling. I had nothing to worry about. The room was warded. Besides, nobody had tried mirror-magic on me in years.

Why's she asking about walls? Sarah's thoughts screamed in my head despite the many songs Sarah had sung to block my mind reading. Usually, her magic worked against me.

She must be seriously worried. I smiled and tried to reassure Sarah—and myself. "I just wanted to make sure on the walls. It's probably nothing, but I just thought I saw my reflection in the mirror move."

Sarah turned toward the mirror, yanking her hair out of my grasp and nearly causing me to lose the brush again. "Without you moving first? Freaky. Is it some kind of magic I haven't learned about yet?"

I regathered Sarah's hair and pinned it up with a simple spell before continuing. Normally, I preferred the manual process, but I did not want to have to keep doing this. "You probably haven't heard of mirror magic because it only works between two individuals who look a great deal like each other."

"Oh, cool. What is it?"

I shuddered. "I don't like to talk about it much. When we were youngsters…Anyway, we stopped. Nobody much liked—"

The awful tingling cut me off. It blocked my vision and spread over my body, dissolving me, squashing me.

I couldn't move, couldn't even cry out to warn Sarah that one of my sisters was trying to trade places with me.

It hurt even more than I remembered.

I fought with all I had to hold my place, to stay myself, but as always, my sister's will (it didn't matter which sister) was stronger. They were always stronger.

I squeezed down into a tiny point and then expanded rapidly back into my normal size.

I opened my eyes with a gasp, just in time to see Matrian, the cruelest, most gorgeous of the boys from my childhood. He brought a giant golden sledgehammer down on a giant gilt-edged mirror that was the only thing other than people in the stone-walled room where I found myself.

The mirror splintered into a thousand glittering shards.

As I shook my head, trying to clear my thoughts, Mat raised his hammer again, and brought it down towards me.

"No!" I shouted, and thrust out a shield, which blew out strong and golden from my fingers, pushing Mat, and every other person in the room, backward towards the walls with such force that they passed out in a wide circle around me.

Well, that was different.

I turned my hands over in front of me. They felt like my hands but had callouses where mine did not. Plus, I'd never managed such powerful magic with my own hands.

I felt almost giddy with the power my sister's body lent me.

I'd never before been quick enough on my feet to make use of a different, more powerful body.

I turned slowly around the room, conjuring golden vines as easily as I'd put up Sarah's hair. More easily. In moments, I'd trapped each of my childhood tormentors.

Except the worst of them.

My eldest sister, Straltia Prima, must be who had gone through the mirror.

Into the bedroom of the Peace Queen of Dicrandia.

And Mat had destroyed my only hope of reversing the change or even warning Sarah.

Sarah would be able to tell the difference and protect herself in time, wouldn't she?

CHAPTER TWO

Sarah

"Nobody much liked…" I prompted.

Straltia shook herself. "The mirror magic. It can be quite unpleasant."

For once, I wished I could read her mind because I could have sworn that wasn't at all what she'd been about to say.

In fact, if I looked at her closely, Straltia seemed odd—different, somehow. She stood straighter, and her eyes met mine with a confidence I'd never seen in them before.

"Are you all right?" I asked.

"Of course. Why wouldn't I be?"

OK, wow. She was deflecting questions by answering them with questions, now? What was she hiding? And why? I definitely needed to do some research on this mirror magic on my own and figure out if it was something I needed to worry about.

And here was where Straltia would normally answer my thoughts despite the songs upon songs I'd written to prevent her from doing exactly that.

"So, are you excited about seeing Phil?" Straltia asked.

Wow. I mean, sure, I was excited to see Phil. He'd been off at the coast for almost a week. But where was that coming from? It didn't have anything to do with what I'd been thinking at all.

It's like Straltia had suddenly become a completely different person.

Was that possible?

If it was, who was the person standing behind me, in my bedroom, holding my hairbrush?

CHAPTER THREE

Straltia

Turning in another slow circle, I took stock of my situation. Three more of my sisters—all confusingly named after my father, just as Straltia Prima and I had been. Besides Mat and the three other Straltias, there were two of Straltia Prima's other fashionable and deadly friends, and six of the large, good-looking, and easily influenced guys Prima liked to keep around for muscle.

It was odd that I couldn't hear them. Every time I'd switched places with one of my sisters in the past, I'd been overwhelmed by her friends' thoughts.

But perhaps, I'd become better at controlling my gift so that I only heard those I wanted to hear. Certainly, I'd been working to both develop and direct my ability for months. With humans, who had relatively unprotected minds, I wasn't sure I was making any progress, but what if I was?

I reached out to the circle, prodding the minds around me.

Unconscious, all. They dreamed of terrors—both mental and physical—that Straltia Prima had inflicted on them. Burning beneath their skin; nightmares just at the edges of their vision, cages filled with their own personal terrors. The pain and fear started to overwhelm me, and I pulled back, shutting them out.

I could shut them out!

I took a deep breath. I might be back in a dungeon workshop in Stralton, but I was not helpless.

I would get myself out of this mess, and I would help the Dicrandians, as they had helped me all those months ago.

One in the circle around me stirred. I inclined my head toward the gorgeous, dark-skinned fae. Bryna had been less awful toward me than many. I might even have liked her if she weren't so apt to turn her considerable potion-making skills toward curses and poisons.

Her eyes opened, and she blinked. *Is she or isn't she?* she thought.

"How can you not know who I am?"

"I'm so sorry, Your Highness," she whispered. "It was just—I mean—Please, don't cage me. I didn't realize."

I narrowed my eyes at her.

"I was so sure you'd succeeded this time. You seemed to flicker, and…" She glanced over at the remains of the mirror. "Mat broke the mirror. We'll have to start again. Please, don't hurt me. I'll do anything. Make the draught of darkness. Or the infusion of influence."

"Why would I need an infusion of influence?" I asked, trying to sound as haughty as my sister would if anyone offered her such a thing. Straltia Prima had never needed potions to magically bend others to her will. She was nearly as powerful that way as our father had been.

It really is her! Pure panic seeped through Bryna's tone, and a whole series of horrible, nasty little tortures flashed through her memory. Straltia Prima had been nearly as cruel to her as she'd been to me.

The panic seemed to waken the large fae on either side of Bryna. They thrashed in their bonds. *What's happening? Did it fail? I thought it worked! But Straltia the Weak couldn't have done this to me.*

I turned toward the dark-haired fae who'd thought that last bit. "The Weak? You dare believe I am weak?" Anger welled up in me, and I felt an uncharacteristic desire to squash this idiot, to visit on him all the years of abuse I'd suffered at the hands of other idiots like him.

It felt wonderful, soothing, powerful, when his thoughts dissolved into a gibbering mess of "So sorry, Prima. Your Highness. My true queen. Of course, you're not weak. Not weak. Never weak."

My pleasure at his fear startled me. Was I turning into my sister in thought and deed as well as body?

Or was this truly me? Had I inherited my father's sadistic streak, just as she had? Was weakness the only thing keeping me from being a monster myself?

Weakness that was no longer a problem for me?

The thought scared me more than the group of fae surrounding me—and they were among the most terrifying people I had ever met.

CHAPTER FOUR

Sarah

Suddenly freaked out by the fae woman who was my best friend after Steph and Gen, I turned in my chair and did my best to act normally. That meant smiling big and saying, "Thank you so much, Straltia. I absolutely love how great your styles look—and how little time they take."

"You know if you ever want to try something new, I've been practicing, and I can do some quite fancy styles."

I snorted. Was she kidding with that? Fancy? Me?

Straltia knew I hated all that elaborate, frou-frou stuff. We'd even had fairly extensive conversations about it.

She didn't seem to remember, though. She stared at me, eager, as if waiting for a response. As if she honestly expected me to suddenly develop an interest in having a sophisticated fairy creation on top of my head.

It was the most ridiculous thing I'd heard all week.

Yeah, no. Not happening.

But I didn't want to hurt her feelings over something that didn't matter that much. She so rarely expressed any kind of opinion of her own. I gave her the brightest smile I could muster. "I think I prefer the simple styles we've been doing."

"Oh, but I could—"

"I'm sure you'd be great at whatever it is, but it really doesn't sound like my style. Now, I've got to run, Straltia."

I couldn't believe she was arguing with me! Straltia never did anything like that. I grabbed my backpack and scooted past her, hoping she didn't realize how incredibly nervous she was making me.

She wasn't acting like herself at all.

I glanced at the fairy-detection feather on my backpack to see if it was showing the presence of a fairy I didn't know or trust.

No alarms there.

Still, Straltia didn't feel like my Straltia anymore. As soon as I was out of here, I was going back through today's security video to see if I could spot what had happened.

And I was definitely going to figure out what mirror magic did.

CHAPTER FIVE

Straltia

I would not be a monster.

I refused.

But neither could I admit to being myself, here, amongst this group that had been tasked with containing me in one of Straltia Prima's torture cages while she accomplished her business in Dicrandia. Sure, I'd managed to knock them out at first, but that was only because I'd caught them off guard. Already some of them were working their way out of my vines and preparing to fight me.

There was no way I could handle all of them at once when they were in full fighting mode.

And that didn't even take into account the officials, guards, and citizens outside this room who considered me a traitor to my country.

So, I'd have to pretend to be Prima while she attempted her mission in Dicrandia. What was that, exactly?

I delved into the mind of the muscled, dark-haired fae who'd called me weak, searching for my sister's plans. Prima had been wise enough not to share many details with him, but even from what she had shared, her plan was clear. She'd taken my place in Dicrandia in order to put Queen Sarah under her thrall, and then destroy Dicrandia from inside out.

This, she felt, would be the best true revenge for the

havoc the Dicrandians had wreaked in Stralton.

Maybe it was.

I however, had no desire to avenge our father's death, or to organize the chaos in his kingdom. The man had been nothing but cruel to me, nothing but cruel to any of his subjects.

His governing style deserved to fall.

Perhaps I could further dismantle his legacy while I figured out a way to escape this place. Again.

I circled slowly, staring at each of my sister's flunkies in turn. They had all awakened now. "Who else doubts my identity?" I asked softly, but with menace lacing my tone. I'd heard Prima use just this voice more times than I could count.

The minds around me quailed in fear as fae babbled their denials.

That is, most of the minds.

Mat's thoughts didn't quiver or quake. His words spoke of fear, and a fear exuded from his body, but it was only skin deep. Inside, he thought, "I know exactly who you are, little traitor."

"Matrian," I said softly. "It seems you need some persuasion."

"You wouldn't," he said.

I barely heard the others gasp as his thoughts dragged us both into a memory of his time in his cage. Pain. Unbearable pain.

I nearly screamed, but in time, I remembered the exercises I'd been working on with Sarah to block out others' thoughts and direct my abilities. I jerked my eyes away from Mat, threw up my mental walls, and directed my mind at the next person in the circle. One of my other sisters. Straltia the Graceful. Grace.

What is she waiting for? Could she truly be Wimpy?

"Who are you calling wimpy?" I growled

"Sorry. So sorry, Prima," Grace whispered. The fear in the back of her mind had lessened, though. If I didn't do something about Mat, I'd be discovered.

I had to send him to his cage.

But I couldn't inflict that kind of torture on another, even to save myself. Could I?

Perhaps I wouldn't have to.

In my mind, I reached past the underground workshop to Prima's room, where I found the cage meant for Mat. It was a masterful piece of work with walls so strong, I doubted any fae could escape without help.

The torture was equally strong magic, but in this new body, I had only a little trouble yanking it out and leaving only the container.

I turned back to Mat, careful this time to keep my guard up and my gaze away from his eyes. "One last chance," I said.

"You're not Prima," he said. Even through my guards, I could feel his certainty shooting at me.

"I guess you need some time in your cage."

He laughed.

I snapped my fingers and sent him there.

Several people screamed.

"Anyone else?"

The mind voices around me had returned to their nearly incoherent terror.

"Enough!" I said. "We will accomplish nothing this way."

I snapped again, and the bindings fell off the remaining eleven. "Get up. I need ideas, plans. And I need to clean myself up." I brushed mirror dust off my shoulder. "We'll meet back here in an hour."

An hour? Oh, I'd hate to be Mat, Grace thought.

I smiled at her. "Some of you had better have some excellent thoughts by the time I return."

Then I winked myself to my sister's rooms, leaving them all.

I could feel their fear trailing behind me, even in the void.

Coming Soon!